To the first men in my life

SECRETS
— *from the* —
BLACK BAG

Susan Woldenberg Butler

The Royal College of General Practitioners

The Royal College of General Practitioners was founded in 1952 with this object:
"To encourage, foster and maintain the highest possible standards in general practice and for that purpose to take or join with others in taking steps consistent with
the charitable nature of that object which may assist towards the same."

Among its responsibilities under its Royal Charter the College is entitled to:
"Diffuse information on all matters affecting general practice and issue such
publications as may assist the object of the College."

British Library Cataloguing-in-Publication Data
A catalogue record for this book is available from the British Library

© Susan Woldenberg Butler, 2005
Published by the Royal College of General Practitioners 2005
14 Princes Gate
Hyde Park
London
SW7 1PU

Designed and typeset Robert Updegraff
Printed by Bell & Bain Ltd

ISBN: 0 85084 302 2

SECRETS
— *from the* —
BLACK BAG

Contents

Preface

Fact is a poor story-teller. It starts a story at haphazard, generally long before the beginning, rambles on inconsequently and tails off, leaving loose ends hanging about, without a conclusion. [1]

Here are stories from, and about, general practice, particularly about isolated, single-handed general practice, across our globe. The stories are based upon interviews over ten years with general practitioners, on top of whose testimony I've constructed fiction.

Who are my voices, my witnesses, exactly? *Secrets from the black bag* presents GPs hurrying through the night from the early to the late twentieth century, from Pakistan to Tanganyika, from Scotland to New Zealand, all over the planet. They carry little black bags into the private worlds of patients struggling with the business of living and dying and trying to make sense of things. A perplexed forester in the Scottish Highlands confronts love for the first time, gun in hand. A rebellious London nurse stitches up an arrogant surgeon near the Benin border. An elderly shepherd wants to stay in his own home with his dog. A Sikh couple in Tanganyika fight the stigma of infertility. Divina's obedient husband Ambrose does not ring for an ambulance during her fatal heart attack. A young woman hides her illegitimate baby under a wardrobe and denies its birth. Mrs Babbadge's anosmia inures her to the mouldering stench of the home she shares with a rotting husband and two frenetic terriers. A five-year-old dies alone in a hovel in the middle of the night, killed by the negligence of a psychopathic stepfather, while a teenager dies of cancer in a comfortable farmhouse surrounded by a loving family. An exhausted thief scrabbles to provide for his massive family and energetic wife.

The doctors speak to us of their delights and fears, their failings and successes.

'The mystery and mystique of house calls is that you don't bloody well know what you're walking into,' says Noose Grimely.

'Has Mum whacked one of the children? Has Dad whacked Mum? Are they going to tell the truth or engage me in a guessing game? Home visits are a fearsome responsibility,' says Zoltan Nagy.

'I was called out one cold night when the stars were out and it seemed that this was an exciting thing to be doing. It was probably one of my first,' says Amaranth Fillet.

'Did the hundred-yard dash. Surgery to Mr Rice's house. Banged at an old house. Peeling paint,' says Hugh Page-Russell.

'The sky there was magnificent at night. You'd smell the gidgee smoke, a scent I'll never forget. So at the outstation there'd be that smoke, the dogs, the people you couldn't see because of the dark and the glow of the fire – and somebody sick,' says Tommy MacDonald.

'Patients would live in a lane in a house with a name but no address. You couldn't see through the fog anyway. There was a tradition of hanging a sheet out over the hedge when you called a doctor. So I just drove along until I found the sheet,' says Dexter Veriform. 'Nobody wanted to know these people.'

'Once, coming home, I saw the Southern Lights ...'

But there is more to this collection than doctors traversing dark nights to patients, bag in hand. The NHS, locums, euthanasia, miscommunication, medical consumerism, the rise of the part-timer; changes in medical practice and patient attitudes over the years; computers, litigation, games patients play with doctors and doctors play with patients; de-skilling, taking time out, ethics and changing ethics, community responsibility for illness; a spiritual dimension to work; alcoholism, firearms, the despera-tion of love, family networks; drug testing by pharmaceutical companies in developing countries; patients who haunt one; what makes a good clinician; third-party intervention into the doctor–patient relationship ... all of life is here!

And the home visit?

'Very often you're going into the unknown ...'

'Dirt road, rough as hell, no lights but your headlights and you're driving along wondering, What am I going to find? ...'

'Home visits? Bloody hell! They can haunt one. The last act in a drama. Blood-splattered linoleum. They're relevant alright!'

A final word on the subject of names: most of them are chosen to be deliberately odd to underscore their fictional nature. Hugh Page-Russell, for example, is a tribute to my favourite landscape architect, the sublime Russell Page. His *Education of a gardener* is a personal treasure. Pretentious *moi*? Transforming him into the military doctor who appears in these pages is naughty. And the rest are simple Tasmanian anarchy.

So a last word to Somerset Maugham:

> *When someone tells you what he states happened to himself you are more likely to believe he is telling the truth than when he tells you what happened to somebody else.* [2]

SUSAN WOLDENBERG BUTLER
Campbell Town, Tasmania 2005

Acknowledgements

Thanks to the GPs who opened their memories; to Rodger Charlton and Helen Farrelly for spoiling me with the sort of civilised publishing experience writers dream about; to Ruth O'Rourke for splendid copy editing; to Robert Updegraff for wonderfully atmospheric design; to Robyn Friend for invaluable advice; to Simon Brown and Ann Bliss for endless reading, as well as to the other readers; and to John Last for encouragement in the early stages – indeed, all the way through.

Special thanks to Alec Logan for believing in this project at the very beginning and pushing it to fruition and for superb editing. I couldn't have done it without you.

Last but not least, thanks to my sometimes patient, sometimes grumpy husband Colin for answering all those medical questions in passing, on the way to somewhere else.

Foreword

Secrets of the Black Bag observes doctors and patients. Then re-tells their stories. Stories located where doctors and patients meet most face to face, in general practice. Where the science that is medicine bumps thrillingly against human fear, passion, despair and hope.

These are not new stories. Many of the protagonists are old or dead. There is a whiff of pipe-smoke on colonial balconies, a sepia-tinted glimmer of grateful patients and be-chauffeured physicians dispensing pills and wisdom of dubious efficacy. There is no political correctness, yet to be invented. And there is the recurring bitterness of the old condemning all that is new.

Are these stories relevant to 21st century general practice? To a shinier but less personalised era? Where personal state-funded doctoring is under threat (and arguably deserves to be) by more modern, cost-efficient, and perhaps profitable models for healthcare delivery? Whither the Black Bag in this new world? But then ...

In 17 years of general practice only one patient has ever asked me to hug her. She was younger than me, and had end-stage alcoholic liver disease. Her abdomen was distended with fluid. I thought that she might die, and for the first time she had realised also that she might die. Her mother had been my father's patient, and my babysitter. I needed to admit her. She was frightened, and as she left my consulting room, hospital admission letter in hand, she asked for that hug. I obliged, I hope not too stiffly.

A week later my partner was called to an unexpected death. My patient. She had spent four hours in A&E waiting for her bed, had become tremulous, and discharged herself. She died alone in her flat later that weekend. Our new PFI-funded hospital has elaborate shrubberies but too few beds. This enrages me.

For Enraged, see *A Lonely Death in the Middle of the Night*, in this collection. For Furious, Amused, Puzzled, Mildly Irritated, Moved, and Profoundly Uplifted read on.

ALEC LOGAN, Deputy Editor
British Journal of General Practice, London, October 2005

The trials of Rosie B

Thucydides Hare

*'You don't mind if I shell walnuts, do you?' asked Professor
Thucydides Hare ('Call me Harey'). He carved time from a
punishing schedule to indulge his passion, baking endless loaves of
improbably coloured sweet breads, using ingredients from his own
garden and orchard. 'Beet loaf, our own beetroot,' he said,
nutcracker in hand and nutpick by his elbow. Harey's proud of
his nuts, which are the size of hard-boiled eggs. He hit a rhythm.
Crack. Toss. Pick. 'So you need to talk to your favourite medical
ethicist,' he said. Professor Thucydides Hare was the yardstick
against which many doctors measured themselves. It wasn't long
before I knew why. Crack. Toss. Pick.*

L ISTEN TO THAT. A computer whirring inside. A **kookaburra** laughing outside. How life's sounds have changed
since I started seeing patients in the 1950s. I'd no idea
the inequities and aggravations of the National Health Service
would drive me to emigrate to the antipodes.

The clack of clog on cobblestone characterised my early years
in northern small-town industrial England. People encased their
feet in thick woollen, hand-knitted socks, over which they wore
clogs to work in the cotton mills and paint factories. These
places were very damp and very loud. People learned to lip-read
to communicate. They'd become so accustomed to the noise
that they talked without speaking, mouthing at each other across
the street with absolutely no sound. Their protracted conversa-
tions were eerie to behold.

The townspeople spoke a language of their own. The lovely
word 'oo' meant your wife. I remember visiting a Mrs Grey. A
chap met me at the door and said, 'oo's a-bed.' He meant his
wife was in bed. The Greys had a small cottage – two up, two
down. A tiny bay window overhung the narrow, winding street.

As with all these houses, the front door opened straight into the front room. The dunny and washhouse were out the back across a stone-flagged yard. Mr Grey led me to a square room with lathe-and-plaster, whitewashed walls. The young Mrs Grey lay dying of a sarcoma of the thigh. I could only administer painkillers; however, this story concerns the mother who now twittered nervously in the sickroom and whose guilt positively suffused that sad night. Poor Rose.

Let me tell you about Rose Ballinger. Charles, my senior partner, said that she called him out one winter's night in the 1920s. The housekeeper interrupted a bridge game between himself and the town's lawyer, the other doctor and the bank manager. That stern woman felt her way through a blue haze generated by the committed pipe smokers to inform Charles of a young lady's excruciating abdominal pain.

Out Charles went into the snow, urging his coughing, sputtering car up the moor toward a tiny village known as *t'owd engine* because of a derelict boilerplate remnant from a long-dead factory. He found the fifteen-year-old daughter of the house in late second-stage labour, obviously about to deliver.

'I'm not pregnant!' she shrieked, screams distorting her black Irish looks.

In these days of boisterous permissiveness, we forget that unwanted pregnancies ruined lives. Still do, in many parts of the world. Our stance on abortion was one of the first things we doctors sorted out. I was quite sympathetic to those poor girls, like many of my colleagues – except for those whose religion forbids abortion. We know the arguments for and against. I'm a healer not a judge.

'What's your name?' my senior partner asked a very frightened young lady.

'Rose,' she gasped between screams.

'I'll be back as soon as I find a midwife and hot water, Rosie,' Charles said gently. He returned to find the girl resting quietly. No baby. No sign of baby. She was flat. That was that.

'Now come on, Rosie, what've you done with the baby?' Charles asked.

'I never had a baby,' she muttered, head turned away.

Charles knew better. He searched the room. He clawed overhead atop the chest of drawers: nothing. He rustled clothes inside the chest of drawers: nothing. Eventually, on his hands and knees Charles bumped a bundle under the wardrobe. He tried to fish it out with his umbrella.

The midwife arrived. All action stopped as the good woman stared.

'I'm looking for a newborn baby,' he said, explaining his undignified scrabblings.

The midwife eyed him quizzically. Not one word escaped her pursed lips.

Charles most certainly yearned for the grunts of male camaraderie, the slap of cards on a table and the puff-puffing of pipe-lighting rituals.

'Ah, here it is,' he announced, pulling the warm bundle from under the wardrobe. The rough blanket caught on a splinter of wood with a tiny snap. He proceeded to unwrap the future Mrs Grey.

Rose married a city boy the following year, who disappeared before long and never returned.

~ ∾ ~

Rose and I participated in one of those curious coincidences that abound in life but lack artistic verisimilitude. Guess who turned up in my new country half a world away and half a century after the birth of her daughter, Mrs Grey? That's right. I had a few more miles on *t'owd engine* and so did she. Back in the nineteen-twenties, Charles's aural associations with Rose had been a rebelliously sputtering car and a teenager screaming denial. Fifty years later, mine would be yapping dogs and vomiting ambulance officers. But I'm getting ahead of myself.

After the death of her daughter, Rose Ballinger must have wanted a new start. Amazing that she came to my particular little spot. She always denied we'd met before, something I felt all the years I treated her. It may seem callous not to remember Rose, but I'd seen her only briefly one night whilst focused on her dying daughter, one in a sea of patients.

Now, half a world away, I was doing the first of what would become my annual locums for a dear friend. I've always enjoyed keeping my hand in clinically, after the remoteness of epidemiology. Rose Babbadge was the first patient I saw. She came in for an influenza vaccination.

I'd happily have gone to see the Babbadges at any hour, so when the dear lady rang through one day on my lunch break I took the call with alacrity. I was about to make what would be my first and last home visit to the usually healthy Mr Babbadge.

'What's the problem, Mrs Babbadge?' I asked, idly thwacking the stack of medical reports before me.

'It's Lennie, doctor,' came the quavering reply. 'I think he's died.' If Mrs Babbadge, alias Rose Ballinger, requested a home visit, things were serious indeed. She thought she could manage all her problems without confiding in another human being.

'I'll be right over,' I said, undoing the top two buttons of my shirt. I don't wear a tie. I don't consider myself socially superior to my patients, which ties can indicate. On the way out I asked the receptionist to send an ambulance round.

I nearly vomited in the Babbadges' bedroom. They say if you work in a chocolate factory, you don't smell chocolate. By such reasoning, I should be immune to whatever my patients throw up. Not so. Mr and Mrs Babbadge were a lovely old couple in their eighties who lived near the surgery. They were both blind. And, with the attrition of old age, most certainly anosmic.

The Babbadges devoted themselves to their two yappy Heinz dogs. The two little angels could do no wrong. Mrs Babbadge led me, palms groping at the walls, into their bedroom. Stupefying. The dogs had shat all over the place. Neither the lounge room, the kitchen, the bathroom, nor their bedroom had escaped. Dog and cat food turned the floor into a minefield. Plastic pet bowls had once contained the food that now trailed onto the carpet in mouldering nuggets and merged with desiccating dog turds. My feet alternately squished on dog food or crunched on God-knows-what. The sharp perfume of cats' pee added another layer. The cats must be out prowling for birds. The carpets were rotten. Every table bore food: old, relatively new, slightly eaten, half-wrapped, fully wrapped or unwrapped. I went for a window. Mrs Babbadge stopped me. 'Please doctor, if you don't mind,' she sighed. 'I do so feel the cold.'

Mrs Babbadge never opened her windows. I respected her wishes, against my better judgment. Really and truly it was appalling. I nearly added a stomachful of vomit to the whole mess.

None of this touched the fragrance of her husband for quintessential putrefaction. As Mrs Babbadge said, a part of her husband certainly had died. His right leg. 'Mrs Babbadge, what's happened here?' I asked, examining the unconscious man.

Mr Babbadge had worked his entire life in the railways, to which he'd sacrificed his left arm in a horrific accident. He'd been big and beefy and still towered over me. His father had invented one of our aromatic cooking staples. That benevolent man had given his fortune to charity and left nothing to his only son but a retirement of squalor.

'I don't know what happened, doctor,' she answered, an edge of hysteria in her voice. Mrs Babbadge had a little bit of blood pressure. She always smelt of urine, as do many old ladies.

'Did he cut his leg?'

'Well, he did trip in the lounge room a while back, on an old tin of dog food.'

'Opened?'

'I think so.'

'I'm sorry, Mrs Babbadge, but he needs to go to hospital immediately.'

The dogs started a new round of yelping as the ambulance arrived.

'They'll take good care of him,' I assured the anxious wife as I headed for the door. 'I'll let in the ambulance people.' I glanced back at the tableau of a blind old woman fussing over her putrefying husband, dogs snuffling at something underfoot.

'Oh, Lennie,' she wailed when she thought I'd left. She covered his face with kisses before caressing and encircling his right paw with her small, square hands. From somewhere deep he responded. He drew her close, murmuring, 'Sweetheart.'

The ambulance officers, a male driver and a woman, wheeled a trolley into the bedroom. Both looked solemn and very green. They started to move the old man. The disturbed bedclothes wafted a new fragrance upon the air. The driver bolted from the room, covering his mouth. A few heartbeats later, the sound of tortured retching reached our ears. I managed to marshal my self-control, only just. The contents of my stomach remained where they were. The other ambulance officer kept swallowing valiantly, in vain: she rushed from the room and added her sweet soprano. Those two little curs nipped at the driver. Soon 'Nice dog,' 'Good dog,' and 'Get down, you mutt!' replaced the wretched retching chorus.

I wanted to laugh at the horror of it all. Turning to Mr Babbadge's leg sobered me instantly. His poor wife looked over-whelmed.

The ambulance officers stumbled back into the bedroom. 'Sorry, doc,' the driver said. His companion summoned a wan smile.

'I very nearly joined you,' I mumbled.

I went back to the surgery, in no mood to work on medical reports. If only Mrs Babbadge had contacted me sooner. Mr Babbadge died in hospital shortly afterwards of septicaemia, his wife at his side. She died about a month later in care. I've seen it time and again, that one partner follows the other. It seems to be a loyalty to the very end, no matter what.

Seeing the Babbadges in their home context earlier would have enabled me to give them better care. Yet what constitutes good care? Is it my perception or the patient's? Squalor may have been the Babbadges' objective reality, but would they have been happier in a nursing home? I think not.

If I'd been less committed over the years, I'd have missed the silent drama of Rosie Babbadge. Who among my younger colleagues would agree to share the responsibility for Mr Babbadge? Most of my older colleagues had retired or were scaling back. Things were different with doctors of my father's generation. Those gentlemen hoped to work until they died. They heard the siren-song of medicine-as-calling, not a part-time job to be left at the end of a shift, potential problems fobbed off on colleagues, problems like pathology results, like emergencies, like palliative care, like work responsibilities, like goodwill generated, like business generated. Nobody worried about equitable pay.

For the doctors of my father's generation, no computers clicked and whined. Kookaburras chuckled, frenzied dogs yapped, wives wailed over dying husbands. Doctors like Charles, committed men all, would have scoffed at personal computers. Charles preferred the crisp snap of shuffling cards and the involuntary grunts of the players in the card game of life.

Eventually the city razed the Babbadge home. Last time I passed, a pizza parlour occupied the site. The smells differed, although the colours reminded me of Mr Babbadge's leg, as did my beetroot bread. The wind moaned like Rosie Babbadge, and no kookaburras laughed.

Eggs and bacon in Alice Springs

Tommy MacDonald

*'You two can call me a runner all you want, but some of us just
don't fit into the stationary medical world, which is turning us
into business people,' said Tommy MacDonald. He poked the fire
with his boot, unleashing a shower of sparks that sneezed in the
vast bowl of night. 'GPs, especially rural ones, spend a fair
amount of time on the road.' Tommy leaned into the light. His
ponytail, more elastic band than hair, nudged his neck with a soft
scrape. 'Think I'll start with some road thoughts.'*

I OFTEN FEEL Dulcie's spirit in the pale ghost gum trees and
the red sand, adding another brush stroke to **Namatjira's**
landscape, when I'm driving to a see a patient in a remote set-
tlement. Maybe she roams the vastness with the **kadaitcha** man
and the spirits of those poor children. Wally did what he could for
Dulcie, and it was plenty. I did what I could for two toddlers, and it
wasn't enough, not nearly enough, and in this country too, not
some third-world hellhole. That's why I get so fed up with patients
whinging about their rights and why I can't take working in the
suburbs anymore, unless it's to relieve some other GP desperate to
get away. And it's one of the reasons I love going to sea, but then I
was born with a love of the sea. Could be my great-grandfather's
wandering genes, but whatever it is, it's got me.

Oh you're lucky, you're lucky being up on the top deck of a
ship at night, alone with the stars and the wind and five miles of
water underneath. Joseph Conrad was right to say that the true
place of God begins a thousand miles from the nearest land.[3] My
need to be out there creates a constant conflict between my own
inner needs and those of partners and children.

It begins a thousand miles from land, or a bit less. Once we were deep-sea trawling twenty-five kilometres out to sea in the Southern Ocean off the west coast of Tasmania, when up from the depths came fascinating creatures you'd never see in a fish and chip shop or fishmonger's. It was a spiritual experience. They had big eyes and large mouths, like octopi and stingrays, but with different shapes from the ones in shallow coastal waters. There were brilliant red spider crabs and electric rays. We pulled up nets full of sharks from hundreds of feet down. About twenty to fifty centimetres long, they were charcoal grey with white bellies. They exploded when they came up from that depth, destroyed by their swim bladders.

Being dragged from the depths, up out of my comfort zone to possible annihilation, seems to be something I do to myself regularly. I'm convinced that the need to test oneself has spiritual dimensions. John Berger thought doctors needed to experience all that is possible, driven by the spirit of inquiry.[4] That's my philosophy, which includes movement with a questing element. Patients are the material of experience driven by the spirit of inquiry, which makes them sacred.

I couldn't avoid the sacred when I entered an Aboriginal community in the Red Centre for the first time. I was engulfed by another kind of sea under the vast sky with night creatures of another reality. I'd finally managed to extricate myself from a medical practice in the suburbs, a process that claimed my third wife. Working with the Aborigines or doing rural locums certainly tests one's limits. You don't have the comfort of backup or a safety net and you learn to face your own fears, unlike the complacency of suburban general practice. You cannot say to a patient in the outback, 'I'm going to ring up the ambulance and we'll chuff you off somewhere.' The buck stops with you.

The questing wasn't just professional. My suburban woes were a lot different from those of my fishing-boat persona. Will the vehicle fall apart on the road? Will my gear fall out? What have I done? Flying into a place for a weekend is not the same as arriving with your bed and your underpants. I've just left my kids and everything familiar and I don't really know what's ahead. My marriage breakdown left me feeling eviscerated, and I now had three kids. I needed to pull myself together.

Driving along in another self-contained vessel on another sea, this one of red dust, reviewing the needs of my children reminded me of two Aboriginal little ones I'd seen recently in the faraway north. I think a lot when I'm on the road and now was no different. The day started like most days in the treatment centre we'd set up in the town hall, an open-plan brick building with a corrugated iron roof. The floodwaters had receded, revealing scattered clumps of seven-foot-high grass. It looked human the way it fell back over itself, and corpse-like in the dry season. I could hear the creek gurgling if I listened hard. Mothers cooed outside the door trying to soothe their crying children whilst a few middle-aged and elderly people squatted patiently, lost in their own thoughts or playing with the children.

'Hold him while I look in his ears,' I said to Mum. The eighteen-month-old on the examining table was a lovely child, with big brown eyes and a sweet disposition. It was heartbreaking to see a mum come in with a desperately ill toddler. All these children would need myringoplasties for their discharging ears, I thought, and they'd all have wet chests.

Mum nodded and looked away. They weren't comfortable with you eyeballing them. Like most people here, she suffered from hookworm anaemia and borderline malnutrition. She scratched at her cotton print dress, which was missing several buttons and hung loosely on her small body.

I bent over the child with the otoscope and found a discharge and inflammation. I percussed the right side of his little chest, which was okay. I percussed the left side, which wasn't. There were creps and pneumonia and other clinical problems as well. He was febrile and dehydrated, with a urinary infection. He had secondary infected scabies, like sixty percent of these people. He'd be lucky if he didn't develop valvular heart disease from recurrent strep infections. The rate here's about seventy times that of white Australia. This and a neighbouring island have the highest incidence of end-stage renal disease in the world, related to an autoimmune response to the streps that infect their scabies.

I heard a sizzle and the lights went out. Shit. Last week we'd spent an afternoon swabbing the floors and fixing the plumbing, a disgrace and nuisance, and now this. We couldn't bring in petrol for the generators because of the petrol-sniffing problem. I'd seen twenty-five-year-old adults just brain dead, the legacy of all that sniffing. Mentally zero. That we had got the treatment centre built at all was a small miracle of organisation and serendipity.

The fizzle of the lights going out and the crackle of the boy's chest reminded me of being out at sea, where the sounds are so different from land ones. The way of the water depends on where you are. Up forward you hear the waves, the forceful pounding smash of water cascading up and over onto the decks. There's the boom of impact and the whoosh of waves, and it's more than just aural. The visual experience of water thrown up onto the decks upsets your balance, and there's the feel of the wind and the spray in your face. Down below decks, the engine predominates with an engulfing mix of vibration and rumble. You're constantly hearing the engine in bigger ships, and feeling its comforting vibration. Astern, the churning tumbling velvety sound of the wash makes me absolutely poetic.

I didn't feel very poetic after seeing a two-year-old girl a few days later. I got to thinking about my youngest child and her mother, my artist ex-wife. She thought I was too self-contained, didn't need her enough. I have to agree, especially after her last exhibition opening. I'm not cut out for cocktails and chitchat. I prefer to be out here, alone in the vast Namatjira landscape, feeling the wind on my face.

I hoped the hours of driving through nothingness wouldn't blunt my mind's edge, my diagnostic and clinical edges. I'd packed the haemoglobinometer and a couple of other things, but everything else depended upon my clinical skills. A sick little trooper lay listless, flat and febrile on the examining table. Her sunken eyes confirmed my fears: pre-terminal septicaemia. I could not send the child off to hospital for blood cultures. I had to get out the heavy artillery. We had some Ceftriaxone, which is pretty potent. Microbiologists would probably say it was over the top, but I had to choose a life-saving intervention from our limited repertoire, whether it was the most appropriate drug or not.

'This child needs to be flown to Darwin, but I have to stabilise her for two or three days before she can be moved,' I said.

The mother nodded.

'We need to get some food into her body. This is faster than by mouth,' I explained, reaching for a drip.

The mother coughed and looked away. I didn't like the sound of that cough. These people have five hundred times the incidence of tuberculosis of other Australians.

Looking at mother and child, I realised that nothing has changed in Aboriginal health in a quarter of a century. The morbidity and mortality are unchanged. The health infrastructure is still inadequate. In this community alone the morbidity is five times that of a comparable population in urban Australia.

There's no easy solution. Education is not enough, especially with the systems currently in place. We need some infrastructure for a start, at the coalface, not supporting the bureaucracy that sits between the bag of gold and the patient. We need modern, well-designed clinics with decent plumbing, X-ray machines and in-patient facilities. That's just pure funding, which is not getting down to the end of the line. What's happening to it? Yet the government spends 2.3 million dollars a year to fly patients like this child in and out of Darwin's hospital. It's an international disgrace. Only the most altruistic doctors would tolerate this bureaucratic bunk.

I got the drip up and the IV fluids running to rehydrate the little girl, and I planned to stay the night to monitor her. That rewarding aspect of medical practice was spoiled by the knowledge that she'll return as soon as she's well and the cycle will start all over again. The ears will discharge again, the chest will get wet again, the scabies will still get infected, the nourishment level poor and the hookworm anaemia present.

Am I really making much of a difference? There's not much continuity of care here, and certainly no continuous care. It would only take six doctors to come here for two months each year.

The child before me didn't cry. She just lay there, watching me listlessly. I did what I could, but it wasn't enough, not nearly enough.

~ ∾ ~

I hoped I could do more where I was headed, towards a reality at the other end of the age spectrum from those two children in the faraway north. They lived in a different world from my own three. The needs of partners ... I was about to encounter a durable partnership that taught me a thing or two. Different limits were about to be tested, and Joseph Conrad and John Berger weren't far from my mind. In fact, there was quite a crowd in the car that night, in the white Toyota camel gliding through the night desert.

I was driving back to the community about ten o'clock after a day of eggs and bacon, coffee and newspapers at the casino at Alice Springs. Usually I had muesli for breakfast in the caravan, so a day in town every six weeks was a welcome break.

'How about a lift, doctor?'

Every time I left Alice, somebody asked me for a lift somewhere.

'Sure, Wally, hop in.'

An old Aboriginal bloke, taller than you'd think, climbed in the front of the troop carrier after settling his wife, daughter and her kids in the back. Wally had the air of self-sufficiency I've always sought. He didn't have to prove anything to anybody. He walked with the earth's heartbeat. Dulcie was right beside him every step of the way.

The way our vehicle negotiated the pitch-black night reminded me of being out in a fishing boat. A small self-contained vessel sailed through the vastness, like nail scissors cutting through a bale of fine wool. Wally's quietness took some getting used to after the banter and chatter of my usual motor-vehicle journey companions. In due course, we came to a T-junction in the road, where a wooden, two-pronged signpost indicated outstations to the right and the community to the left. I turned left, lost in my own thoughts.

On a night like this, I could understand why Aborigines believe in sorcery and spirits. It's a mistake to say that the world's oldest known religious culture, one that dates back over forty thousand years, is primitive. Religion gives shape and meaning to every aspect of Aboriginal culture. Underpinning their worldview is the Dreamtime, which refers to both the time of Creation and the present. Nature is the sacred *Thou*, with form, substance and willpower. Nature herself is not sacred, but the residence of Ancient Beings who inhabit every part of the landscape. People aren't just human bodies, but possess spirits that come from the Ancestor Beings. We commune with these beings through intermediaries, stories and sacred places. Three spatial dimensions plus the Dreaming compose Aboriginal reality, so it's quite possible to communicate in an invisible reality with an invisible spirit. As in other ancient religions, insubstantial concepts possess the same value as objects of form and substance, and may be personified, so for instance evil spirits personify evil.

'Who was that?' Wally whispered as I drove past the signpost.

'What do you mean?'

Wally didn't say anything else. I didn't pursue it. Three generations slept in the back.

The next day I had to see a sick child at the outstation whose turnoff we'd passed the night before. During the day this panorama by Albert Namatjira, the Aboriginal painter, revealed red sand, white ghost gums and blue undulating hills studded with red and orange rocks. The brightness of the sun, the immensity of the sky and the flatness of the landscape were quite disconcerting after the compact, misty green three-dimensionality of the valleys and mountains of my home.

I got talking to some of the people, who said, 'The *kadaitcha* man was here last night.'

He's a spirit that can travel vast distances quite quickly. He can come in and not leave any tracks. The *kadaitcha* man wears emu feathers on his feet so you don't know if he's coming or going. One meaning of *kadaitcha* is evil.

'Last night, four of our men tried to track him,' someone said.

Wally had seen the *kadaitcha* man and I had not. The Ewe-speaking people in West Africa believe that the soul leaving the body provides an opportunity for a wandering, homeless soul to enter. Is the *kadaitcha* man an invisible being or is he a skilled astral projection of a soul from a living being? Perhaps he's taken over the soul, but where's the vacant body? Perhaps, all alone with the stars and five miles of sky above.

Not hectoring Wally about the *kadaitcha* man was the culturally appropriate thing to do. If I had, I doubt our friendship would have developed so readily. Certainly the trust-child vital to a doctor–patient relationship would have been born severely retarded.

I did things there I would never do with my patients in the suburbs, like hunting wild bees and **echidnas** with Wally and Dulcie. Wild bees, *cooba*, are non-stinging black insects a bit smaller than our summer fly. They build hives in hollow branches in trees parasitised by termites. You need an axe to get at the *cooba*. If you're lucky you can spot their entry and exit hole and observe them coming and going.

'Sugar bag,' Dulcie said, using their name for the honeycomb.

At the top of the hive the cone is almost full of a dark honey with a beautiful flavour, whilst at the bottom are the eggs. They burst in your mouth like caviar with a contradictory sweetness between the honey and the little pop of the egg, which is bitter like a vitamin C tablet. If some of the bees get stuck in it, you eat them as well.

'Tracks, over there,' Wally said one day, looking at the sandy red ground. Two white ghost gums stood nearby, independent yet reaching towards one another, like Wally and Dulcie. I hadn't attained that yet in my own relationships with women.

We set off toward a pumpkin-coloured rocky outcrop.

'Porcupines,' Dulcie said, pointing to an echidna disappearing into a hollow log in the riverbed about fifteen feet long. They're quite territorial.

'Use this,' Wally said, handing me a stick. The intense blue of the sky tinged his white hair.

I poked and prodded, but the echidna wouldn't come out. Wally had a go.

'We'll have to use this,' he said and chopped out the far end of the trunk with an axe.

We killed the echidna and cleaned it by putting it whole in the ashes of the fire. This burnt off much of the spine and hair. The rest Wally shaved off with an axe, revealing pink skin like scalded scraped pigskin. Wally nicked the abdomen and pulled out the guts. Dulcie scraped away the campfire, placed the echidna on the hot sand and covered him with more sand and coals. After an hour's cooking the echidna tasted very nice, its dark brown juicy meat a bit like native hen.

Dulcie and Wally were healthy enough to be hunting well into old age, untouched by the many infectious diseases ravaging their community. Leprosy and tuberculosis were absent here, unlike the northern settlements in which I'd recently worked. But other infectious diseases appeared, like pneumonia, nits, intestinal worms and such secondarily infected skin lesions as boils and infected scabies. Also present were the usual colds, runny noses, trachoma, conjunctivitis, ear infections, diarrhoea and gastroenteritis.

One year I found Dulcie curled up on her mattress like an echidna. A crippling stroke had taken her health. Her daughter, the one who rode with us in the troop carrier the night Wally saw the *kadaitcha* man, came to her mother unbegrudgingly. The family didn't insist on moving Dulcie to suit individual convenience. Dulcie's home was a **humpy** with four pieces of forked tree trunk stuck in the ground and two crossed members. That supported a few sheets of tin, four feet high by six feet wide, providing shade from the heat of the forty-degree centigrade days of summer. Hung from one of the forks was an empty twenty-kilogram flour tin from which protruded bread and meat. The dogs couldn't reach it but the crows could.

People don't live alone there unless by choice. I'm struggling to recall anybody who lived alone, but I can't. People shared possessions, money, food, shelter – everything. They lived in houses or humpies or slept on the ground outside. Some walked shoeless one hundred or one hundred and fifty meters over hot sand to get water for drinking and washing, returning with buckets of water and trying not to tread on rubbish.

This was an appalling situation in which to look after someone. Dulcie lay on a mattress on the dirt, which her daughter had swept, wearing her usual jumper and cardigan over two dresses. She couldn't talk or move and I don't think she recognised me. Her daughter sat next to her, giving her water from a chipped mug and food from an old enamel bowl. She brushed the flies away from the old woman's eyes and mouth. Before long, the family would bury Dulcie's body in the bush. They wouldn't hold a public mourning ceremony with intense grief and self-mutilation, as when a young person died. They'd dismantle and destroy her humpy and burn her bedding and clothing, and that would be that.

Wally didn't talk about his wife on subsequent hunting trips and I didn't ask, but I saw the way he looked at the ghost gums.

Pizza delivery!

Zoltan Nagy

'Some of us have been called upon by a higher power to participate in the eternals of human life,' said Zoltan Nagy, red-faced and puffing like a cherub in the corner of an antique map. He ping-ponged through the crowds of tourists consuming beignets and coffee at a Jackson Square café in New Orleans. The smell of impending rain stifled us, along with the fug of wall-to-wall people and the heaviness of frying doughnuts. 'It is the difference between a calling and a job, as some part-timers view medicine these days,' he said. 'Can we wonder at the lack of respect shown us by any patient under forty?' He deposited our grub on a table. 'Thrilled you could join us for this conference, pet. This is one of my favourite cities.' A child shrieked for pizza at the next table. 'Ah, pizza! That reminds me of a home visit.'

ME KID'S SICK,' said a disagreeable male voice. 'My address is …' Down went the telephone. No request to come, no directions, just an assumption I would drop everything and go. I knew this type: bit of stubble on the lower jaw, matted dirty blond hair, surly blue eyes, a way of walking from side to side that said, 'Give me a wide berth.'

Fortunately I knew the area pretty well. Since a child was sick, I went immediately. I would not have gone for an adult.

I banged a closed fist on the knockerless door. Damaged guttering, chipped paint and riotous weeds bespoke long-term neglect by residents of the two-bedroom weatherboard cottage. A television's blue light flickered through the bay window on the right. I doubted they could hear me above the din.

I did not know what I would find, as any police officer can tell you.

Many types of patients request house calls. It is the same everywhere. There are the ill patients who have left it longer than they ought. Nobody minds about them. They apologise for bothering you and hate to acknowledge their illnesses for a variety of reasons. There are the total wastes of time who think only of themselves and their convenience – like Mr Penborth. Our newest associate had rung to request that I do a home visit for her. She was on call but disinclined to take on the Penborths at home.

I pounded on the door again. No one answered so I stepped inside. I had done so many home visits in houses like this that I knew where to go, even without the television's cyanotic hint. I opened the first door on the right. Everyone smoked and lay around on the floor watching a video.

I was spot-on about Dad. Add a pasty complexion and pained expression. I could not muster any compassion, even by recalling the games powerless people play with authority figures, which usually works for me. This is the end result of medical idealism, I thought sourly. Health for all by the year two thousand, the United Nations dream for the developing world seemed farther away than ever, although that year was fast disappearing behind me and this was the developed world. The concept has come and gone.

The place reeked not only of cigarette smoke but also of clothes long unwashed. A five-year-old boy, obviously unwell, lay on a grimy blanket in front of the television.

Mum, the *de facto* Mrs Penborth, stretched out in a corner, drinking a beer. ''Eahr, 'e's over there,' she said, not moving a muscle. She was as tall as her man and twice as broad. Whereas Mr Penborth had a square jaw, Mum's meandered all over the place and quivered with the effort of moving its various chins out of TV-lock position.

Mum had dressed the sick child in a T-shirt and filthy shorts. No socks, no shoes, despite the cold. The most common reason I have been called out at night is for a child who has taken ill during the day and has not got better as the parents had hoped. If it has gone to sleep at all, it has awakened screaming. The parents want to know what is what.

I could not hear anything as I began my examination, so I switched off the television.

'Oi. What in the 'ell are you doin'?' demanded a belligerent lump on the floor.

I looked at the miasma whence arose these words. 'I am going to listen to this sick child and you're going to be quiet until I do.'

The kid had an earache and needed Panadol and sympathy, so I said to Mum, 'Who is going to go to the chemist?'

'Bloody 'ell,' Mr Penborth said, 'whadya wanna go to the chemist for?'

'Because the kid is sick and he needs some medicine, *now*.'

''Aven't you got nothin' in your bag?'

'No.' There is a rule I always keep: if you get me out at night, you go.

'Can't it wait 'til the morning?'

'Look,' I said, 'I am out, he is sick, you go to the chemist.'

'Bloody 'ell,' Mr Penborth said. 'I'll miss the video.'

'Everyone can wait until you come back.'

'Oh. Well, I 'spose I'll 'ave to, won't I?'

'Yes, you will, because I am not leaving until you do!'

Eventually, muttering all the way, Mr Penborth disappeared out the door. He returned in due course. I administered the medicine and prepared to leave.

No one doubts the enlightened, compassionate nature of universal health care. My medical colleagues would be appalled were I to suggest something I've come to believe over the years, that certain patients should be forced to pay, at gunpoint if necessary – not a very humane attitude perhaps, but one borne of desperation. Allow me to digress. One unfortunate end-product of socialised medicine is an anti-doctor bias culminating in doctor bashing and, in extreme cases, murder. I've observed noticeably less respect for our profession over the years, particularly since socialised medicine appeared. Not that I am a male chauvinist, but I do believe it is silly and dangerous for young female doctors to go out on certain night calls.

A lump on the floor near the door moved, enabling me to avoid stepping on it. 'An' 'oo's the fool,' it asked, meaning I worked while he lay enjoying a video and drinking beer.

I left. I crossed the tiny veranda under rusting grillwork, opened the thigh-high iron gate with my fingertips and negotiated a footpath buckled by the roots of a giant eucalyptus.

Thankfully, I had spared our associate the Penborth visit. They're the ones who make house calls unpopular, but the child should not suffer even more. I arrived home in a foul mood, I can tell you that. One needs to release that pressure somehow. I hectored my poor wife. 'Pick pick pick,' she said, 'like a fly buzzing an oozing scab.' She was watching a video, *Fried Green Tomatoes*, some sort of cooking nonsense. I declined to participate.

The welfare system stripped Mr Penborth and his cronies of initiative and self-respect. If I had dug deeper, I would have uncovered depression under all that belligerence. On the positive side, Baby Penborth will not suffer from Absent Father Syndrome.

Looking in the same direction

Yam Peale

'Those years in Africa were the happiest I've spent professionally,'
Yam Peale said. Church spires and stained glass rose behind us
towards the heavens as we poked through the graveyard. 'They
were hard years for Centuria, in terms of respect and recognition
and the day-to-day realities of life. I was often away at clinics
during the week and only home on weekends.' Voices raised in
praise drifted amongst the tombstones. 'Centy made many
sacrifices for God, like most of the mission wives. Invariably
patients stopped by at the weekend, so we had very little time
together and with the children, especially when they were babies.'
He bent, read the inscription on a gravestone and frowned.
'Babies remind me of Africa, babies and spirits.'

W E DESPERATELY NEED a doctor,' Dr Graves told me
over cream of mushroom soup in London at a mission
fundraising dinner. 'I'd love to go back to Central Africa,
but my wife won't let me,' he added with a resigned glance to his left.

I looked at Centuria. My guardian angel played with her food
absently. That meant she had something on her mind. Had the
meaning of this dinner moved her as it had me? Did she realise
that urban general practice was not my calling?

We had no children yet. If I read my wife correctly, we would
soon be on our way.

I did. We were. That night God changed the path of my medical career forever.

We left our familiar London landscape of shining lights and lin-
dens for hurricane lamps and those wild baobabs that look
upended, as if their roots are in the air. I'd be practicing a different
sort of medicine as well, although some problems are universal.

Nothing worried the prosperous young Mr Singh, not the
epidemics and pneumonia nor the meningitis and diarrhoeal disease that accompanied runaway population growth in our city.

People were deserting the countryside for regular running water, education for their children and employment other than endless peasant farming.

Centy and I were there at the time of a demographic shift from land to grand. Expectations led to gross overcrowding. As fast as we provided housing, sanitation and health services to one area, a new one rose nearby. Our city, on a plateau of four thousand feet should have had quite a healthy climate.

None of this worried the young Sikh in the slightest. He wore his usual pink turban, white shirt, khaki shorts, knee-length stockings and work boots. He never shaved; soon he would be able to divide his beard in the centre and twirl it up the sides of his jaw, like his elders.

'We're having a baby,' said Mr Singh, bounding into the surgery like a large dog and skidding to a stop. 'I want you to look after my wife and deliver our son.'

'I cannot provide that service,' I said. I knew that Sikhs liked to deliver their babies at home. If anything went wrong I would never be able to live it down. Being new I couldn't afford any mistakes or failures.

Mr Singh prowled the consulting room benevolently, picking up this and examining that. He listened politely as I explained my reasons for not delivering babies in the home.

'We'll look after your wife here in the mission hospital,' I said, 'or she can go to the government one.'

'I'd like you to deliver my son at home,' Mr Singh said, twirling the steel bracelet that Sikh men wear.

'I will not take on that responsibility,' I replied sternly. 'I want to make that quite emphatically clear.'

'Ah,' he said, chuckling, 'but you will. You will, doctor.'

'I will not.'

Mr Singh laughed heartily and left.

Over the next few months, whenever Mrs Singh came in for checkups, I told her in a voice that brooked no opposition, 'You are going to the mission hospital to have this baby.'

She did not reply.

The crush of professional and domestic obligations engrossed me. I forgot about the Singhs.

We were in the city now, which Centy found easier as we had children of our own.

One afternoon, an old Sikh man burst into the surgery.

'You must come quickly doctor,' he said with great urgency. 'Very ill person. Must come very quickly. I think person dying.'

I grabbed my medical bag and ran for his Jeep. This old man in a blue turban drove me down into the town, laying a forearm on the horn at every opportunity. His sense of urgency increased to fever pitch with every laying on of the arm. My ears were ringing when he finally braked hard, without slowing down, in front of a woodworking shed.

Sikh craftsmen were the backbone of the technical and skilled services in our city. They did nearly all the work in the hospital – building, forging, carpentry, motor mechanics. Africans perceived the manufacturing and technical skills of the Sikhs to be valuable to the community. Of the other resident Indians, Hindus ran the shops. People perceived them to be valuable as well. They viewed as exploitative the entrepreneurial skills of the Ismaelis, who were Islamic rather than Hindu and revered the Aga Khan. Most Ismaelis left for America and Canada.

No one could have mistaken the old man I followed at a dead run for anything other than a Sikh. His blue turban unspooled a path between benches and tools, weaving round stationary bent heads. Saws and planers buzzed. People shouted and threw bits of timber past the machinery. We dived through a few open doors and crossed a quiet little courtyard towards a house.

A tall, hefty Sikh woman stood waiting. She treated the old man like an irritating insect, dismissing him with a voluble harangue whose meaning was unmistakable. All of his self-important urgency deflated under her tongue. He aged twenty years as he slunk away, spent after passing the baton to this matriarch.

'This way, doctor,' she said, gesturing with a regal nod of the head. She sailed into a room with a low bunk bed three-quarters surrounded by a light muslin mosquito net.

Several other large females busied themselves in the room with women's business.

'There she is, doctor,' they said, pushing me towards the bed.

Before me lay a young Sikh woman obviously in labour. A fair bit of blood stained the white sheets. I didn't recognise Mrs Singh at first. She wore a long shirt over a pair of voluminous, white pyjama-like trousers that had blood all down the front of them.

Mrs Singh groaned. I did a quick assessment of what was going on. I felt her tummy. Empty. She can't be in labour, I thought. She's not in term. I looked down in the genital region. More blood. She moaned as something disappeared down one of her trouser legs. I reached down to investigate and pulled up an umbilical cord. Great. Up came the placenta. I followed it down the other trouser leg and found a baby, which I pulled out. He squawked a bit. I did the necessary.

I'd come out with only my bag, so I had nothing with which to tie off this cord. I looked around; providentially, a sewing machine sat near the window. Sikh bedrooms always have sewing machines. I reached into a tangled pile of elastic and threads and bits of tape, extricated something useful and tied off the umbilical cord.

By this time the Sikh women had gathered round and were smiling profusely.

'Here,' I said, handing the baby to one of them.

'Thank you, doctor, thank you.'

'Yes doctor, thank you very much, doctor.'

The new mother smiled at me. I smiled back.

Everybody was happy.

I walked across the courtyard towards the whine of buzzing saws and planes. Bounding towards me came the proud father.

'Have a drink with me, doctor, to celebrate.'

''Fraid not. I've got to get back to work.'

Mr Singh looked at me solemnly for a moment, then broke into a big grin. 'See,' he said, 'I told you you'd come.'

I had been conned, well and truly. As the outcome was so successful, I didn't mind. That boy is grown up now.

We had a meal with the family last time we were back there, a few years ago.

$\sim \infty \sim$

Another little boy was not so lucky. Never was a baby more loved than Mrs Mbabze's.

'Thank you, doctor, thank you very much,' said Mrs Mbabze, gathering up her baby. Another child crouched listlessly nearby while a third tugged at her black, hand-woven sarong.

'She's just the height she should be for her age and weight,' I said with satisfaction. We were in a mission hospital in the highlands, in the village of a paramount chief. All round him, for fifty miles, radiated his tribal area. The first mission hospital, set up in the 1890s, had expanded from a tent under a baobab tree to a few iron sheds to a few mud-walled buildings to concrete structures with iron roofs, which still were quite primitive.

Recently I'd introduced the idea of charting height-for-age and height-for-weight graphs. Mrs Mbabze was one of my favourite mothers. She took a keen interest in the material we gave mothers to monitor their babies' growth.

'Bring her in next month and don't forget her card,' I said. The fat healthy babe had her mother's liquid eyes and quizzical eyebrows.

'I won't, doctor,' she said, nuzzling her youngest child.

And Mrs Mbabze would not forget. These mothers were pretty good about bringing their children's cards to post natal and child health clinics.

I hoped this baby would not go the way of so many others. Often we charted children's progress from healthy to desperately ill. They started in the green, healthy part of the graph, with an appropriate weight for their height and age, then wavered and headed through the grey area into the red section, where weight-for-age was far, far too little.

A thunderclap boomed overhead, heralding the rainy season. Often a healthy child veered off course when the malarial season started. In those days, malaria – chronic and recurrent – was the biggest single factor in child mortality in those highlands. Add to the brew other illnesses such as tuberculosis and meningitis, and it was not surprising that forty per cent of children died before the age of ten. In England a general gloom pervaded a hospital in which I worked whenever a child died in the paediatric ward. In that part of Africa children died while you were doing the round.

One year, four hundred children died in our mission hospital.

The satisfaction I felt at the progress of Mrs Mbabze's fat babe disappeared with one look at her listless toddler, headed for pneumonia at the very least.

I bent down and examined him briefly.

'If he gets any worse,' I told Mrs Mbabze, 'bring him in immediately or send for me.'

'Yes, doctor.'

People had ten, twelve, fourteen children and lost four, five, six of them. The cause could prove difficult to trace. A child might die of pneumonia, but he may have had severe malaria for two or three months and become anaemic and frail. Another child might die of what appeared to be malnutrition. He had access to adequate food, but other causes had made him ill and he wouldn't eat the food. Protein-energy malnutrition was common, in which a child eats virtually nothing but water and porridge. Although the recorded cause of death would be acute diarrhoea, a recurrence of malaria or a chest infection, it was next to impossible to unravel all the contributing factors.

Practicing medicine in Africa was totally different from practicing in the West. I saw only major pathology, trauma and disorders and such illnesses as tick fever. People were very poor and drugs difficult to get. They didn't hoard or waste medication, like my former patients who ferreted away large amounts of antibiotics and other drugs. The outside toilet of one lady I visited in London overflowed with unopened bottles of forgotten pills.

I dragged my mind back from its unpleasant reverie. As a Christian, I should work to help people in poverty and strife in any part of the world that needed me. Watching Mrs Mbabze shepherd her babies through the rain, I felt a wave of love for my own wife, now pregnant with our third child. We'd agreed to stay in Africa until the time came to educate our children. We couldn't ask them to sacrifice their education. How fortunate I was to have a supportive wife who allowed me to follow my dreams, indeed who shared them. As Saint-Exupéry said, 'Love does not consist in gazing at each other, but in looking outward in the same direction.'[5]

No Nose and the rabid dog

Hugh Page-Russell

'Sex shop. Things are not what they seem,' said Hugh Page-Russell. 'Stride the aisles with me. Yeah, interesting merchandise. So you like that one. Uncircumcised. Actually it's a torch. Press here to turn it on. Head pops out and lights up.' The door to a nearby cubicle banged shut. The ex-military man's head jerked up. 'Sound reminds me of the tetanus ward in Pakistan.'

W OULD YOU BE so kind as to examine the gentleman holding his epigastrium and moaning, Dr Page-Russell?' A voice coughed gently in my ear. 'So sorry to disturb your repose.'

''Course,' I said, jolted into wakefulness.

That was then. Not like now.

Fifteen years of unremitting general practice. There's enough now for the kid's education. We can sell the beach house. I need some time out. Maybe do remote locums. Had a look through a Médecins Sans Frontière brochure last week. But I love my patients. Some of 'em. Feel responsible for all of 'em. There's more than one kind of time-out. Like the Muslim prayer room some friends have in a Malaysian surgery. It's a small room with no posters on the walls. No magazines. Or ads. Just the right to have time out during the day.

I lurched awake last night. Hugged the wife. Whispered from a hypnopompic fog. I didn't want to silver in a world of funny turns and tablets. She didn't wake up. I dream of returning to Pakistan. It was a different sort of time-out. Little squirt of altruism that possesses some people and doesn't usually last long. Especially when the pay is twenty-eight dollars a month and a potential spouse waits back home. Went to Hunza first, in the far north. It borders China, India, Afghanistan and Russia. Hunzakuts live productively to great ages. Always dreamed of tasting their glacier milk. Still feel the sand in my teeth from that grey water.

Thought about arriving in the country's capital on the trip out of Hunza. Flew in not long before. Nobody there to meet me. Supposed to be. Bad organisation. Third-world international airport at 2300h. Usual thoughts. 'Oh f***. I'm surrounded by beggars. They've all got their hands out.' Tried to get through customs. Brought six monstrous cartons of syringes and gear which was donated by aid organisations back home. Paid corrupt customs people a fair whack. All I wanted was a drink. Only legal place a multi-national hotel in the capital. It was full of overseas businessmen and expense-account salesmen hawking medical supplies and unnecessary technological advances. And overpaid aid officials in lush linen suits. Sloshy fat asses. Inebriated condescension. Drove up the price of a beer, let me tell you. I soon discovered the terrible home brew. Grain-based like whisky. Bloody terrible. Shocking. So different from the West. And the noise! Dogs barking and fighting. People barking and fighting. Machines barking and fighting.

Weariness overcame me one night in the doctors' lounge of the thousand-bed philanthropic hospital built and run by a wealthy industrialist. Probably jetlag. Two dreams ran together. The first dream was a Mughal miniature. Three women fussed over me, like those three Persian lasses who founded Hunza with three deserters from Alexander the Great's army. That one's personal. The second dream was a Brueghel triptych. I awoke from it with a start. Nightmare about a rabid dog and No Nose, the beggar in Lahore. A huge fungating rodent ulcer had completely eaten away his nose. He hung around the main banking district of Lahore. Banks paid him money to go away. To be that bad in Pakistan at that time you'd got to be pretty bad.

The nightmare scrambled images of city and country. No Nose and the rabid dog ran through the bazaar, which was choc-a-block as usual. Essence of Asia. A tube of toothpaste squeezed between rows of clenched-teeth shops. People oozed through cramped laneways. A dog with a tawny coat parted the river of people like the Red Sea and walked right down the middle, mangy and howling. People were too terrified to approach him. I love dogs. Hated to see endemic rabies.

How different from the countryside. Camels. Sheep. Goats. People dried cow dung in rows of brown pancakes flat in the dust and piled 'em like haystacks. Transferred 'em to a rickety wagon. Laid an interlocking pattern. Like the architectural lacework in the Taj Mahal. An ox carted this edifice to market. The sari of the stacking woman. Blood-red with thousands of pus-coloured balls. A man near her wore white. He rolled up his sleeves to the elbows and draped an orange shawl over his left shoulder. They bent and lifted those patties under a hazy bronze sky. Stiff yellow grass dotted the treeless landscape. Like the balls in her sari.

A voice coughed gently in my ear. 'Dr Page-Russell.' Hauled back to consciousness. I'd been dreaming about the eight-foot security wall encircling the hospital. Keep out the many dogs? Time for a hospital purge. A terrible business. Rounded up all the dogs they could. Shut the hospital gates. Large sticks and much yelling. Chased the dogs into the pukka, a huge pool used for washing, fishing and swimming. Then waited. The dogs got so exhausted they paddled to shore. People clubbed 'em to death by the dozens. There's my Pakistani colleague.

'So sorry to disturb your repose, sir,' Dr Shah said. 'I've got to attend a pregnant woman in complications.' Neatly trimmed beard. Neat crisp clothes encasing his tight little body. Neatly settled between youth and old age. 'Would you be so kind as to examine the gentleman holding his epigastrium and moaning?'

''Course,' I said, jolted into wakefulness. Their approach to emergency obstetrics was destructive. It was aimed at maternal preservation, often at the expense of the child. Women dropped their kids in the fields and went back to work. Presentation at hospital indicated obstetric catastrophe. Infant mortality two hundred and fifty per one thousand.[6]

'Transfusion?'

'Yes, Dr Page-Russell, and I have made the necessary arrangements.'

Patients had to pay for two things only in this hospital. Blood and a deposit to remove the body if they died. Taking blood, you often got a serous-like pink fluid. Everyone had hookworm anaemia. Slides and pathology reports of haemoglobins down to one. Never seen an Hb here less than 3.5. There, transfusion's from a professional donor. Patient, Hb three or four, pays. Imagine the donor's Hb. Usually six or seven. A primitive chemistry laboratory made all IV fluids. Pyrogens gave everybody fevers.

Hurried to the accident and emergency ward. Moans led to a clean-shaven man in his late forties who looked much older. Skinny. Wore white pyjama bottoms. And a long top. And a little Muslim hat. The Hindu industrialist did not push his religious beliefs.

'This is Mr Ibn-Amir,' said the male interpreter politely.

'Dr Page-Russell,' I replied.

Mr Ibn-Amir tried to smile. Teeth stained liver-coloured by betel. He was weak and lethargic. In too much pain to talk. Those days, many Pakistanis had massive peptic ulcers, relating to their constitution. Diet. Stress. Religious-based fasting. Everything was conducive to ulceration. No H2 antagonists to reduce acidity in the stomach. Wouldn't have been able to afford 'em anyway.

'Pain?' I asked.

Mr Ibn-Amir understood and nodded. His cleanliness struck me. He smelt musky and smoky. Cooking over open fires.

'Long?' I asked Mr Ibn-Amir through the interpreter.

'About twenty years.' Mr Ibn-Amir didn't know what it was like to feel normal. Common. Malnourished people and all other accompanying morbidities.

I shook his stomach gently. Mr Ibn-Amir caught his breath and winced. I checked for gastric succussion splash, elicited by shaking the abdomen sideways. All I could do. Sign of gastric obstruction. Rare in rich countries. Only in poor countries would a disease get so advanced I'd use gastric succussion splash as a diagnostic tool. Never seen it since in the West. Don't look for it if a patient's already dying.

Back then in Pakistan that whooshing splash indicated severe pyloric stenosis. Resulting from chronic peptic ulceration. One of our criteria for operation. No role for radiology in the clinical work-up. Most surgery at the hospital was for peptic ulceration. We put Mr Ibn-Amir on the operation list. Sent him to the general ward. Next to the tetanus ward. No one who was admitted there walked out. You need respirators to survive tetanus. None there. We had to be careful closing the tetanus ward door. Sudden noises precipitated acute tetanic spasms.

Wonder what happened to Mr Ibn-Amir. He was forty-nine, which was the average life expectancy there and then. He wouldn't change his diet after the operation, so his ulcer would keep eating into his epigastrium. Futile to expect people to change their habits.

It was like seeing all those rare conditions in Bailey and Love, our old surgical textbook, come to life. In all my years, I've only seen one case of secondary syphilis and none of primary or tertiary. In Pakistan I saw clinical cases of syphilis every day.

Circumstances trapped Mr Ibn-Amir. I was much more fortunate. In two more months I'd be back home, eager to jump on the treadmill. Far away from destructive obstetrics. The doomed patients on the tetanus ward faded into dreamtime fodder, like No Nose and the rabid dog.

Still dream of returning.

Death by budgerigar

E Manley Dew

Tree-song crunched in the canopy far above, trunk against branch. The treetop fringe sported a bad haircut, rambling and rigid against the sky. E Manley Dew's graceful hair rolled and waved inside feminine clips. One would trust this hair to look after one in sickness and in health. Fern skirts encircled the smooth trunks of ghostly gum trees. Black cockatoos squawked in the distance. E ('E for Esmee') Manley raised her head and inhaled deeply, mouth and eyes closed. 'Ah,' she said. 'I need this after dipping into that other reality, the professional one.'

NOT BOTHERING THE DOCTOR runs in Mr Blesser's family, even though his budgerigars were killing him. 'That it?' I said to the boss one crisp spring day. The receptionist nodded.

'See you at two, then.'

Morning surgery had been long. I'd come in early to stitch up a chainsaw accident and hadn't stopped. I looked forward to Mother's lovely hot vegetable soup.

Something shiny wedged under a box of tissues caught my eye. It was a plastic card in an old torn wallet. Mr Blesser had forgotten his Repat card.

He didn't live far. I had just enough time to drop off the card and drive home to do justice to Mother's soup. Mr Blesser was a Vietnam veteran with a very bad chest. He didn't smoke but had an incessant cough, which had brought him to see me earlier that morning. We'd had a great old chin wag but hadn't solved the problem of his cough.

No one answered my knock. I heard something round the back – a sound I soon identified as Appalling Coughing and Budgie song. What a sight, a real aviarist's wonderland! Mr Blesser had stacked cages stuffed with budgies from one end of the garden to the other, creating Mondrianesque lines across every surface. Shadows danced and birds fluttered.

Of course! Mr Blesser had psittacosis, a disease parrots transmit. Budgies are parrots, after all. How had I missed it? I knew the answer. I'd lowered my index of suspicion, something easy to do when you see people regularly year after year. 'Mr Blesser, you didn't tell me you had budgies.'

'You didn't ask,' he replied, coughing that dry awful cough.

'We've got to get you on antibiotics immediately.'

'Tomorrow, doc.'

'We must get you seen to right away.'

'I just bought these new budgies, doc.'

'You didn't breed them?'

'Not this time, doc. I wanted to introduce some new bloodlines.'

'Well, they must have brought in psittacosis. That's what's wrong with you.'

'I'll pick up them antibiotics at the chemist in the next day or two.'

'Is your wife still with her sister in Sydney?'

He nodded, seized by a coughing spasm that was terrible to behold.

'Look, Mr Blesser, if we don't treat this you could die of exhaustion. We've got to get you to hospital.'

'I'm a bit busy now, doc.'

I recalled Mr Blesser's father, who easily qualified as my most stubborn patient. Getting him to give up his driver's license had proved impossible in the end, even after his last funny turn at the wheel of his car. He'd lost consciousness, drifted across the main highway and crashed into a parked caravan. After endless consultations with the local police he finally accepted a license limited to town and the Anglican graveyard, so he could visit his wife.

'I'm sorry, Mr Blesser, but it's very infectious,' I lied. He ignored me.

I'd never diagnosed psittacosis before. For some reason I hadn't asked Billy Blesser whether he kept parrots, which I always ask people with incessant coughs. Only because he left something in the surgery and I took it round was I able to diagnose his nasty illness.

'Mrs Blesser wouldn't be very happy to come home and find you in hospital.'

'Oh alright,' grumbled the aviarist, surprising me with his easy capitulation. He always lost some of his spark when his wife went away. 'But you'll have to get them for me and bring them 'ere.'

Everybody knew the chemist closed for lunch until 1.30. I looked at my watch. So much for Mother's soup.

Win some, lose some

Dexter Veriform

'Unlike my friend Thucydides Hare, I always get personally involved with my patients,' said Dexter Veriform. 'He says he does, but he's too busy doing what's right. Perhaps I wouldn't have come to this, being locked away behind bars ...' He snapped his hands back at the wrists, rejecting evidence of his incarceration. A muffled clank stressed the desperateness of his environment. 'Some of my old patients have stood by me. Others just stand there grinning, as Bob Dylan said. Don't look so surprised. I adore poetry, in whatever form it takes. My patients were full of it, positively overflowing, like "Daown by the barrrn to the caoos ..."'

I ALWAYS HAD a soft spot for that farmer. They called him Wiley Riley because he believed the blether of every travelling salesman. For a week he'd extol the graces of some new gadget or other, then nary another word. He had a special graveyard where he laid these apparati to rest. In the barrn. It was like that in rural New Zealand back then.

One morning in Caesar, the telephone went off at two minutes past six.

'What's the matter, Mr Riley?'

'Well, doctur, the caoo slipped the calf, so I lost a pedigree animal.' His accent was a mixture of Scots and goodness knows what.

'Yes, but what's the point of this call?'

I could hear him scratching his hair, long and curly as his sheep's. 'Well, doctur, the sheepdog got the pedigree spaniel into pup.'

At the end of a long story about the spaniel and the working dog, the farmer added, 'Would you come daoon and see the wife? I'm going down to the barrrn to milk the caoos, and then there's the mare.'

By this time thirteen minutes had passed. 'Can you come to the point, Mr Riley?' I didn't try to hide my impatience. My patients see my every mood.

'Well, doctur, the wife's a bit crook.'

'In what way?'

'She's in bed, bleedin' a bit, and I'll be daoon at the barrrn so I won't be able to bring her up to see you. Just when you're coming daoon this way, would you call in?'

Now, to the farmer, coming daoon that way could have meant any time during the day. Some instinct ordered me to go at once. Your own instincts are vital in the country, because farmers can be casual. I did that six miles in six minutes. Mrs Riley lay in bed with a pool of blood, having a miscarriage, surrounded by three children under ten years of age. I fired her off to hospital. She needed a transfusion and a D and C.

We all had a narrow escape. Instinct told me to go immediately. If I'd taken my time, Mrs Riley would have been dead by the time he got back from the barrrrn. Like so many farmers, Wiley had his priorities: the cow slipping a calf, the pedigree dog in pup to a sheep dog, the old grey mare foaling and oh yes, the pregnant wife.

'Now, if this happens again, Mr Riley, get me immediately,' I said sternly. I remain immovable on the topic of showing emotion in front of patients despite many discussions with Thucydides Hare. Our own vicissitudes affect how we respond to patients, he says. If a doctor's second wife has just left him and his bank manager has called in his house and his business partner has left and he's feeling fairly bleak, then he might have a difficult time dealing with someone else's emotional crisis. Maybe that doctor should be aware of what's happening to him and not take on responsibility for that sort of case, I retort. Maybe he or she should say, 'I can't help you at the moment, but I can send you to my partner or arrange for you to see someone appropriate.'

In Caesar, about a week later, that someone appropriate was the vet. I stopped by the farm to check on Mrs Riley. It was the day the bull fell sick. I hadn't noticed the farmer's prize bull when I'd left the car, my mind full of concern for the missus. I thought I'd parked on the other side of the fence from the bull. Must be upsetting for poor Mr Riley, I thought as I retraced my steps towards the car later, just look at how frantically he's waving his arms. Perhaps I misjudged him.

Then I stopped dead in my tracks.

Now, as the local doctor, I should have been able to drive off in a dignified manner, smiling and waving benevolently. Unfortunately, every ounce of Mr Riley's biggest bull eyed me from near the car. This prize Jersey was a twenty-five hundred pound pedigree animal. He stirred up the soil with one hoof, snorting through the huge copper ring in his nose. I must have been dreaming when I parked so close to the brute.

'Rrrrrr,' the bull growled in the lowest possible rumble. Now, the Jersey is a lovely cow, creamy-coloured with a black muzzle. There's nothing more beautiful. She'll come up to you to be petted. She's a gentle soul. I could weep over the Jersey cow. She is gorgeous. The Jersey bull is a different kettle of fish entirely. His androgens are exceedingly strong, and he shows it by what's between his hind legs.

A very worried doc wondered whether he'd make it to the car. I edged closer, always keeping sight of him. He spared me.

'I don't think your bull likes me, Mr Riley,' I said to the farmer, who had come running. 'He's so angry.'

'It's the car, doctur,' he replied. 'And he's crook. Vet's comin'.'

'Ah,' I said. 'I should have realised. Motor cars frighten him.'

'No doctur, your car scares the shit out of him.'

'Mr Riley!' I protested, loyal to my machine

'It reminds him of the vet's car. Same colour. The vet was here last week.' I remembered hearing in the pub about that case of bull bloat.

As we stood talking, the bull took a turn for the worse. Now, in Caesar I overlapped with the Australian vet whom, fortunately, Riley expected shortly.

'Doctur please help us, he's me best bull,' Riley said.

'But Mr Riley, I don't have the proper equipment. The vet will be along any moment.'

'Wait here, doctur,' Riley replied, loping to the barn at top speed.

The bull and I stared at each other distrustfully. I had my hand on the handle of my wife's Mini, ready to hop inside at the slightest provocation. Riley returned before long brandishing a probang, a special long, flexible rod with a piece of sponge at the end. In those days vets inserted this instrument down the throat to let the wind out.

'The vet left it here,' he explained.

I was trapped. 'I'll have a go but you'll have to help me,' I said, feeling a bit surly. Riley hadn't once inquired about his wife's health.

Riley managed to get the bull's mouth open. I inserted the tube. All went well, with the bull deflating nicely.

My mind began to wander, flooded by thoughts of my wife's cooking.

'Glunk.'

Not a good sign.

'Gulp.'

Even worse. Normally we held our end of the probang quite tightly. For some unfortunate reason, the bull swallowed it.

'Quick!' I screamed.

Riley was already running toward the barn.

'Get me something to open his mouth!'

Riley's face creased into ecstasy. 'I have just the thing, in the barrrn ...'

Oh no.

I sweated, I'll tell you that. I didn't know if Riley had insured that bull for its full value or how long it would take me to pay for it with a ruined career.

Riley ran back brandishing a clamp-like implement. 'It'll hold his mouth open. You reach in, is all.' I must have looked sceptical, because he added, 'The vet left this, too. We've been through this before.'

I should have known. I'm afraid I wasn't as easy on that bull's mouth as I'd have liked. It was my first time. I was nervous. Using that special tool, I prised and held open the bull's mouth. I didn't know what to do next, besides praying for the arrival of the vet.

'The vet puts his arm right down the gullet.'

I growled and closed my eyes for a moment.

The bull groaned.

I took a breath and slid my left arm down his throat. Damned if he was going to get my working arm. I trawled my medical texts mentally. Had there been a noted one-armed doctur?

My arm slid further into the bull. He didn't like that. Neither did I. Finally, I managed to pull out the probang. Riley returned it to the barn for the next emergency.

'Thank you very much, doctur,' Riley said, walking me to my car.

'Your poor wife needs some attention,' I said severely.

Just then the vet pulled up and jumped out of his Jeep, grinding his mangled cigarette butt in the dirt. His Great Dane and terrier trotted by his side. 'Great timing, huh mate?' he grinned.

I grunted and got into the car. 'Goodbye,' I said. I fiddled with car keys.

As I opened the window to give him a piece of my mind, the vet yelled, 'For Chrissakes, shut yer bloody window!'

I looked over, straight into the penis and balls of the Great Dane lifting his leg to pee. I cranked the window shut, praying it wouldn't jam. I'd started using my wife's Mini after meeting a farmer headed the wrong way on a one-way gravel road, driving a load of hay from his paddock. He took out the wing of my big car from the headlight to the front door. That Mini used to take me twice as long and make me twice as tired. I got the window up.

The Great Dane calmly finished his pee.

All ended well. I saw Mrs Riley and cured a case of bull bloat. I have to say, though, that the farmer's wife sticks in my mind a lot less than that Jersey bull's gullet and the Great Dane's genitals.

I snort when Harey suggests erecting barriers to protect myself. I roar when he mentions compassionate detachment and paw dangerously when he waves that red flag, saying that emotional involvement with patients might bias clinical judgment. Reason is not enough, I inform him. If I'd been the soul of detached equanimity, I'd have lost a patient. Instead, I listened to my intuition and saved Mrs Riley.

My intuition saved one patient, but the life of another slipped through my fingers, quite literally, as I held him in my arms. The worst possible thing is when a patient commits suicide. Poor Mr McLean.

One Sunday afternoon before Christmas, a call came to meet the ambulance at a nearby farm. Blast these Sundays and holidays! They make people crazy. Second shooting in two weeks. In the first, one young man had been told mistakenly – not by me, thank God – that he had a particularly nasty stomach cancer. He didn't want to be a burden to his wife so he jammed a shotgun under his jaw and pulled the trigger. The men use guns and they are mostly successful. The post-mortem showed no sign of cancer. How much should the family be told? The local medical community was still grappling with that one when I was called out to Mr McLean.

I'd never met the man despite my involvement with his lovely wife and daughters, so I can't blame myself for missing his signals. Mr McLean was one of those healthy farmers who kept away from the doctor. I knew the type and suspected the reasons for his action. Wool prices, his children's schooling and the drought had dragged him into a corner of his land he preferred to avoid: letting go all but one of his men, whose families had depended on his for generations, watching the land parch and his wife's face pinch.

I stuffed plasma, oxygen, the ruddy lot into the car and raced through the streets and into the surrounding farmland. Somewhere a siren wailed. I broke just about every traffic law, swerving around slow-moving tourists in every permutation of vehicle, self-propelled or otherwise. The town's population had swelled like a sponge, absorbing holidaymakers on a seaside sojourn.

Now, attitudes towards firearms are cavalier in rural New Zealand and Australia – as in most country areas, I suspect. A while back I stopped going hunting every year. I must be one of the few people round here who is anti-gun, simply because I know that if anything happens I'm for it. I'll be the one called out, like that Sunday morning that a farmer climbed through a fence and pulled his rifle after him by the muzzle. He survived a shot in the stomach but it meant resuscitating a chap in a panic, putting in a drip, getting the ambulance and going with him for the three-hour drive to hospital. My wife was not impressed, as she'd planned a family picnic.

Firearms and impulsive behaviour can be a lethal combination. There are all sorts of impulsive behaviours. Shopping is one, but it's not dangerous. Some husbands might argue that point. Arson's another, in certain circumstances. Certain suicidal gestures fall into this category, making a definite argument for gun control. We had a young chap once who tried to commit suicide with a shotgun, but it didn't go off, to his great relief. By some stroke of luck there was no bullet in the breach. He then swerved off in his car, got pulled up by the cops for dangerous, drunken driving, yelled and abused them and got carted off to casualty. He stayed in a hospital bed overnight and a prison cell next afternoon. He returned to work Monday after a bizarre weekend. Little did I know I'd end up in a prison cell myself.

These thoughts of guns and desperate men filled my mind as I turned off the main road toward the McLean place. I jumped out of the car and raced to the farmer's side. He'd chosen a tree behind the barn, not visible from the house but overlooking the fingers of headlands reaching into the sea. I knew that some people felt trapped by all this beauty. Another time I may have felt entranced. The ambulance arrived just after I did. I scowled and was left alone with Mr McLean. He'd put a twenty-two rifle between his eyes and pulled the trigger – and lived. Death was inevitable and we both knew it. The bullet lodged between the lobes of his brain but hadn't knocked him out.

I will always remember his eyes. By the time I got there he couldn't speak. He just looked at me, pleading with his eyes for me to save him. Clifford Beers said the delusion that drove him to a death-loving depression vanished as soon as he leapt out of a window.[7] Mr McLean obviously felt the same, released by the commission of his horrific act.

There was nothing I could do.

'How can I help?' I cried.

Mr McLean just looked at me, speaking with those eyes.

I cradled him in my arms. 'I wish I could do something, Mr McLean,' I said, voice cracking. I wanted to intubate him because his respiration was going down, but something stopped me. I just sat there, holding him.

What would Harey have done? My good colleague talks about Louisa May Alcott[8] volunteering as a nurse in a Civil War army hospital. Once the arrival of eighty ambulances awakened her in the grey hospital dawn. The sight of those hopelessly wounded men led her to admonish herself that she had come to work not to weep or wonder, so she corked up her feelings and returned to the path of duty, something she found very difficult. I could relate to that. One young soldier worried about a gunshot wound through the cheek and what on earth Miss Josephine Skinner would say. Louisa May controlled her risibles and assured him that Miss Josephine would admire his scar if she were a sensible girl. Harey's better than I at controlling his risibles.

Mr McLean's eyes stick in my mind. They shouldn't, but they do. Those eyes were pleading, 'Help me. I've done it, but I don't really want to go.'

I just sat there, holding him.

Now, Mr McLean seemed quite a decent chap. I regretted that this act formed the sole basis of our relationship. The dying process took about half an hour for the poor man. Thirty slow minutes in which I was powerless. Thirty short minutes out of a lifetime that will go with me to my grave. I laid him down gently. Would being uninvolved have made me better able to comfort Mr McLean? Would being distant from my patients make me a better doctor? All I know is that Mr McLean's eyes will haunt me forever. I couldn't save him and God knows I wanted to.

When children die

Noose Grimeley

*'My brother says I've always been inconveniently passionate,
since the wounded birds, stray dogs and elderly farm animals of
my youth,' Noose Grimely said. 'As I was saying, one thing
really ticks me off. When you do house calls nowadays, they don't
even turn the bloody television off. I can't have the thing on when
I'm trying to take a history or listen to somebody's heart. Kids
run in and out of the room. I have to shut the door and say,
"This is a medical consultation. I won't allow all this crap to go
on in my surgery. Why on earth should I put up with it here?"
Kids,' he said, reaching for the bottle of whisky in his bottom desk
drawer. 'There's nothing worse than when children die.'*

I T STARTED AS a typical morning at the surgery until the
receptionist put through a call. 'Can you go out to the
O'Connor place, doc?' asked Lance Smith, a local policeman. 'A child has died.'

'Sure,' I said. I hate it when children die and the authorities
call me in to pick up the pieces. My partner was stitching up a
chainsaw accident so I had to go.

'Another thing, doc. Better take the four-wheel-drive.'
Warning bells should have rung.

I got directions since I didn't know the place. Had never
heard of it in fact, which was unusual. I thought I'd found every
corner of the countryside.

The place was up the back of nowhere. Even the people who had
farms nearby didn't bloody know about it. I drove down a rough,
rutted, rarely used road to a real humpy-looking place, thrown
together from planky-looking wood. No one had painted the place,
which looked roughly made and totally incomplete. In the yard sat
one old car that went and one old car a fraction worse that didn't.

An absolute psychopathic know-all opened the door of this hovel, a manipulative good-for-nothing bastard, not even the father of this child. He'd recently been released from prison. I knew of this man by reputation, because my senior partner had looked after his father when he died. Tattoos covered every visible surface on the man before me, who was pushing thirty. I once knew a psychopath whose cherubic looks belied his essence. This asshole, though, looked beyond redemption. Whatever was handy went into his body: needle, bottle or nipple. Behind him cowered a pushed-around woman, skinny and mousy with stringy blonde hair.

'Where's the child?' I asked.

They stood aside to let me in and pointed to a bundle on a makeshift bed in a dark corner.

Two older children sat nearby, playing with a baby. There's always a baby to consummate the union.

'He had asthma,' the psychopath said authoritatively. The old scenario. We see it so bloody often. These people didn't believe in doctors. They of course knew everything and none of the doctors knew anything. 'We know all about it. We treated it,' the psychopath said. Often the stepfathers kill these children.

'What happened?' I asked.

'We gave him some candle vapours to sniff last night,' the psychopath said, 'then we went to bed.'

Presumably drunk and stoned, if my nose was correct.

'You left him up, with a candle?' I asked.

'Yeah, sitting by the fire.'

The poor little lad had obviously had bad pneumonia, with half his chest full of pus. He pulled a blanket over himself and died. One jab of penicillin would have given that child a good chance of living.

It's awful when children die, just awful. One of my colleagues nearly broke down when a two-year-old drowned in the river. The drowning of a twelve-year-old girl haunts another. Her twin brother apologised in a newspaper obituary. He didn't mean what he'd said that morning, that he didn't like her. Poor, poor child, to run guilt alongside his grief. Yet he was fortunate compared to this little boy.

The poor child died a lonely death in the middle of the night in a bloody hovel. It was just so pitiful. This dead little kid was only five, and about the size of my two-year-old. That he died alone bothered me, without the comfort of even a toy animal. With his last bit of strength, he dragged his filthy little blanket across the floor and crawled into bed to die alone. When people die, they want the basics of companionship and love, not high-tech intervention.

They killed that child. It would not occur to these people that they would be at all responsible. I made four calls to child welfare, who never followed it up. Later I got distressed phone calls from the family of the real father, but what could I say?

That was one of the few times I haven't been able to bounce back to work. I went home and had a cup of tea. I still think about it. I'll never forgive that bloody psychopath who killed his stepchild because he knew more than the doctor.

Less than an hour's drive but more than a world away, Angus Easton died a different sort of death surrounded by loved ones who'd done everything possible to ease his suffering. Angus was obviously the apple of the family's eye, and no wonder: he was a terrific bloke. I brought him into the world shortly after I started here and very sadly saw him out not long ago. One of my first home visits had been to his grandfather, an elderly farmer dying of chronic obstructed airways disease. Trouble with the breathing apparatus is a terrible way to die. His lungs were gradually packing it in. His family were round him all the time. Every visit I made, somebody from the family would be sitting beside him. I learned then about the marvels of extended families in rural settings.

Angus was sixteen years old, with everything to live for. One Saturday afternoon, a teammate kicked him during a football game at their school. He fell down. Luckily, the school doctor was in the audience with his son. 'He's taking a long time to get up,' the man said to his son. 'He's obviously not okay. I'd better have a good look at him.' So the doctor pulled Angus off the field and ordered a CAT scan of his head. Very good move. Very bad news. Angus came home after that.

As Angus' family doctor, I had to perform a duty I bloody well dreaded, one that's never got any easier. Poor Angus was too ill to come in to the surgery. I thought about the little boy in the humpy who died a lonely death in the middle of the night. No way would I give him the news over the phone. His parents were willing to come in for the diagnosis, but I felt that Angus should hear it first, alone. As I headed down the avenue of hundred-year-old elms lining the drive to the farmhouse, I thought about how unfair life is, to do such a dreadful thing to such a nice boy. I usually enjoyed the drive and had a particular liking for the Eastons' Georgian homestead, perhaps because of my fondness for the family. As I rolled to a stop that day, I didn't feel the usual leap of gladness in my heart as Matey, Angus' Gross Munsterlander, bounded to my side. The Eastons had bought him as a guard dog, but he never barked at strangers. The raucous peacocks that scuttered across the gravelled circular drive performed that function better. Matey never minded being out-performed, and in fact got on quite well with the birds.

I couldn't postpone it any longer, so I got out of the car. Mrs Easton came running out to meet me. 'Oh doctor,' she said anxiously, 'We're so glad you've come.'

I tried to smile, unsuccessfully. Bloody hell. She knew. We didn't exchange words. Those were for Angus.

'We're all gathered round Angus, waiting for you,' she said weakly, her voice quavering. 'May I get you a cup of tea?'

'I don't want to trouble you, Mrs Easton,' I said humbly. I can't think why some doctors are arrogant. My patients always humble me with their courage.

'No trouble, doctor,' she said, rallying a bit in her role as hostess. 'We're all having something – although I do wish the girls wouldn't drink so much cola, it's so bad for their teeth,' she continued. I let her chatter. As she led me into the house she added, 'Angus asked me to make your favourite cheese scones. They're just ready to bring up.'

'I know,' I replied, swallowing hard. 'I can smell them.' I didn't want to tell her that they set my tummy rumbling, because it shamed me to think that I could respond to food at a time like this.

'You know where he is,' Mrs Easton said. 'Go on up to his room and I'll join you shortly.'

The poor woman needed time to compose herself or perhaps delay the inevitable, so I didn't offer to carry anything. I trudged up the stairs, round the corner and down the hall. I could hear muted laughter. 'I'll soon fix that,' I thought grimly, opening the third door on the left.

Angus lay in bed with his two younger sisters on either side, holding his hands. Jane had just turned thirteen. Juliet was fourteen. Mr Easton paced at the foot of the bed, trying to hide the emotions conflicting his heart. The daughters were genuinely happy to be tending their brother, in that sublime way of children. I reflected for the thousandth time, how different boys' rooms smell from those of girls. Angus wouldn't be needing the soccer ball or cricket bat spilling out of the closet.

'Thank you for coming all this way to see us, doctor,' Mr Easton said warmly, coming to greet me with his hand extended. 'We appreciate it.'

'Not at all,' I said. 'Angus, how are you feeling?'

'I've been better, doctor,' he said quietly. He wasn't wrong. His blue eyes clouded with pain, but Angus didn't complain. It wasn't in his nature.

Mrs Easton entered bearing a tray of tea, cola, scones and sweet biscuits. Her husband went to help her. He placed the laden tray on the desk, on top of some important-looking school papers. No one noticed. After Mrs Easton served drinks and food, everyone got into position to hear my news. Making sure that people seat themselves appropriately and comfortably is a necessary ritual, I find.

'Angus, are you certain that you would not prefer to be alone to hear what I've got to say to you?' I asked, wishing I had better news.

Angus shook his head bravely. Poor lad.

'We're a close family, doctor,' Mrs Easton explained need-lessly. I could see that in their body language, Mr Easton's hand on his wife's shoulder, she stroking her son's head, the sisters still holding their brother's hands.

I blew on my tea to cool it and bit into a cheesy scone, which didn't taste as good as I expected.

'Angus,' I began. 'I want to be completely honest. You have a tumour of the pineal gland, which is right in the centre of the brain.'

Dead silence ensued.

'What's the prognosis?' Mr Easton asked gruffly.

'Not at all good, I'm afraid,' I said reluctantly.

'You mean I won't be taking over the farm from Dad?' he asked, only half joking.

I put the scone on the blue willow-pattern plate. I had no right to eat it. 'You won't be here this time next year,' I said gently. I couldn't bring myself to say that he wouldn't make Christmas.

I didn't turn in the direction of the stifled sob from his father.

'That knock on the head–' Mrs Easton began.

'– caused a haemorrhage,' I finished.

'He's always been healthy. We'd have noticed,' cried the dis-traught elder sister.

'You could very well be wrong,' Mr Easton said. I know he didn't intend the remark to sound so rude.

'Please feel free to request a second opinion. I don't mind in the least. In fact, I sincerely hope I'm proven wrong,' I said, and meant it.

Angus had not said a word.

'I'm sorry, Angus,' I said.

'Thank you, Dr Grimely,' he said softly.

I'll never forget the look of incredible relief on that face.

'Don't hesitate to ring me at any hour, Angus,' I said, prepar-ing to leave the family alone.

Pulling away from the house, I grieved that Angus would not see another cycle of those glorious elms. His relieved expression appeared before me. Terminally ill people prefer honesty. If they don't they're usually in denial, something that most certainly did not apply to Angus.

I saw quite a lot of the poor child for the rest of his short life. We got him all sorts of radiotherapy, which did absolutely no good and made him lose his beautiful silky blond hair.

One day I went out to the farm. Angus had lost his sight. His younger sister sat on the bed, one leg up and the other on the edge of a chair. She stroked his face while he talked on the telephone. The room was fairly large, conveniently, as it would soon accommodate the various paraphernalia required to keep Angus at home until the end. A signed photograph of a rugby star had pride of place on the dresser. Into a corner of the frame, his father had thrust a small photograph of a healthy Angus playing rugby.

'No sir, pine is fine,' Angus said into the telephone. 'I don't want a lot of money spent on it.' His sister whispered something in his ear. 'Please ring me back tomorrow,' he said. 'The doctor's just arrived.'

'How are you feeling today, Angus?' I asked as he replaced the receiver.

'Well, doctor,' he replied with a tired smile, 'It's obvious I'm going to die. I've been arranging my funeral.'

The girl whimpered.

Angus groped for his sister's hand. She grasped it immediately and held it to her face, biting back tears.

I couldn't do much but prescribe medication for the pain. 'Angus, I'll call in and see you in a few days. Ring me before that if you need anything, anything at all,' I said.

Angus nodded silently and closed his eyes.

As I left, I looked back at brother and sister, so filled with love for each other, and swallowed hard. Bloody cancer.

Angus deteriorated rapidly. Every time I went out, one of his sisters was sitting with him. They never left him alone. Mrs Easton was just great. Mr Easton was out all day with his sheep, but he and his wife took it in turns to stay up with Angus at night. Seeing the system work well is inspiring, when everything falls into place and everyone works together, even though the outcome is bloody awful. Angus' mother fed him through tubes, which my partner and I had to take out and put back again two or three times a day. One of the local oncologists supplied everything we needed. The district nurses were wonderful. Angus stayed at home rather than going into hospital, because that's what the family wanted. The Easton family lived quite a way out of town. They'd have found it extremely difficult to tend both house and farm and care for Angus as they wanted.

Over a period of six months, Angus became deaf and wasted away. The family were not terror-stricken, as sometimes happens, nor did they try to exclude Angus because they themselves could not handle it. I was privileged to see that family at its most magnificent.

It was one of my saddest and yet one of my most uplifting cases. I was just so bloody impressed with the whole family. Every time I hear my colleagues debate the merits of telling the truth to terminally ill patients, I think of Angus Easton's look of incredible relief when I gave him the worst news a doctor could possibly give a patient. Every time I eat cheese scones, I think of brave Angus and his wonderful family. I've never forgotten him.

One night the phone rang at three am

Christy Grimeley

*'You know what it's like,' she said, slurring her words. Her voice
was barely audible above the Saturday-night merriment of a
weekend conference – doctors away, doctors not on call, cramming
it all into one night. She wasn't a foot soldier in the natural
fibres and no make-up brigade, no, Christy Grimely marched in
the silk-and-style squadron. She tapped the flats of her fingertips
on a marble table the size of a generous quiche. The diamonds on
her hand glinted in the dim recessed lighting. 'You'll never believe
what happened to me this afternoon,' she said, clutching the
underside of the table. 'There's no escape.'*

A HAND GRIPPED my shoulder from behind, not so much
a grip as the landing of an alien life form.
   'Yo. Mrs Doctor.'
Oh no.

I was walking along the foreshore, looking out to sea. Another
half-hour to kill before the afternoon session was over. I wasn't
thinking anything special, other than wondering if the sky would
cloud over and I should have worn something heavier. My mind
shifted into neutral on its way down to park, where I hoped it would
stay for the rest of the weekend. I needed a break. So did Noose.
The sea just crashed and crashed, wave after wave after wave.

'Fancy your bein' on a noliday too. Life o' Riley, you got.
Where's yer 'usban'?'

Oh no.

'Ey?'

The stench of cigarette smoke, fried fish and rotting teeth
formed a well-known trinity.

Oh no.

'I need 'im.'

I flicked away the claw with the back of my fingers and turned.

Oh yes.

'Me an' the kids's visitin' me sister.'

Deep breath. Count to three. Make it to one-and-a-half. 'He's off duty, Mrs Meecham. You'll have to find someone else.'

'Whaddya mean? He's took a noath.'

I backed away from enlarged facial pores framed by frizzy, bottle-black hair. 'You need to contact the local GP.'

'No. I wants yer 'usban. 'E knows me. You tell 'im. It's me ticker.'

'You really should contact the local doctor as soon as possible,' I said and headed back up the beach. Maybe one day I can say what I really feel. *You're breaking up my marriage, you bitch. Why can't you just move and take your subculture with you?*

Her voice caught me before I could reasonably pretend to be out of earshot.

'Caravan park. That's where we're at. See he comes.'

I never told him. Should I have? It's one of the things we doctors' wives have to deal with, no right answers in the life-and-death game. Sometimes we make informed judgements to protect our husbands, and sometimes it's an uninformed groping to protect ourselves, although we can never admit this. We've got to shield ourselves, sometimes from our husbands. They need somebody safe to explode at, especially when home visits come at the end of a long day.

I brushed a weak trickle of tears from my cheek. I thought I was cried out.

If I could change anything it would be home visits. Every time Noose's called out at night or on the weekend, he discovers new depths of spousal extravagance. I wonder if it's generational. My father and uncle don't mind being called out, oh no, they just don't mind at all. Maybe I should talk to my mother and my aunt.

I tell myself, Girl, you *could* leave, but it's not that easy and I'm not so sure I want to, even if staying destroys me. So much for women's lib. For better or worse. What would happen if I did leave? What happens to women in general when they take off? Lifestyle degenerates. Incomes plunge by seventy-five percent. And besides, as my mother tells me, we're not women in general, we're doctors' wives. They need us in order to function. I know Noose needs me, but he's got this self-contained side that would manage perfectly well without me. I say that, but it's not entirely true. Noose needs to blood-let. He needs to provoke me into losing control, into anger or tears or throwing things. It's the only thing that relieves his tension. Then he turns deadly calm and smirks at my storminess. He won't allow himself to lose control. It's not done. But society accepts men provoking their wives. Then revisionist history kicks in, no matter what he says. 'All I suggested, in a reasonable tone of voice, was that you might care to review your spending habits.' Asshole. I giggle. 'Asshole of heroic proportions does not become you,' I mimic.

All those middle-of-the-night calls on the hospital phone are sending us demented. The blast of that ancient black monster sets our teeth on edge at the best of times, but at three in the morning it's the stuff of nightmares. Most of the calls are unnecessary. Sometimes it's the incompetence of a night nurse too inexperienced and fearful to make proper assessments, silly questions regarding medication that could wait 'til the morning. I'm not blaming the nursing sisters. Most of them are wonderful, just fabulous.

Whether Noose goes out at night or not, he's still awake and the adrenaline's flowing, so he roams the house like a caged animal. If he can't sleep I can't sleep, so we're both up for hours. The worst is when he's called out for something trivial. He always goes. He never asks if it can wait 'til the morning. 'If it could have waited, they wouldn't have rung,' he says. 'It might be something serious this time.' He doesn't want to miss anything and doesn't intend to be sued.

Most GPs are like this, I imagine. One patient corners me in the supermarket to tell me about the time Noose came with his jammie bottoms showing. I don't tell her that he left home calling down the wrath of ages upon her head. Her child has asthma partly because both she and her husband chain-smoke and are too ignorant to make the connection. She uses my husband as a convenience. I think she'd find it could wait 'til the morning if she had to pay for the service. I'm expecting a conflagration when he finally tells her off, which he keeps threatening. Instead of doing it, he discovers yet another of my extravagances.

Noose's fine when he gets home after what feels like an eternity but is only forty-five minutes. He's worked off his anger, seen a sick child and comforted an anxious mother. His reputation as 'Dr Kind and Caring' etches its way a little deeper into local mythology. He then prowls until he exhausts himself, spreading the smell of second-hand cigarette smoke throughout the house. We finally get back to sleep around five o'clock. Forget lovemaking. Not an option. Invariably the morning sister rings at seven, sanctimoniously horrified that he's still abed the lazy so-and-so. Why do people feel that getting up early is a universal virtue? Not every profession needs to utilise all available sunlight.

Noose didn't have to marry me, you know. No one held a gun to his head. And no, I wasn't pregnant. I didn't realise how tortured he was. I just thought he was complicated and deep, you know, all that stuff that goes with hyper-intelligence. After we got married he started blaming me, first for little things then for all his problems. He picked at me, day after day after day. He never told me that a new dress looked nice, he just accused me of being extravagant, even if I bought it with Christmas gift money. I should have purchased a cheaper dress and used the rest to pay bills or better yet, used it all for bills. I could never do anything right despite working and contributing a little bit to the mutual kitty. A very little bit, he said. The longer Noose has been in general practice, the worse it's got. The boys are older now, and he's never forgiven me for sending them to private school.

One time stands out in my mind as particularly awful. The phone rang at three o'clock in the morning. Whoever thinks all doctors are self-sacrificing saints, ready to leap from warm bed and wifely body into the cold night, has never lived with Noose. He is anything but happy to have his sleep disturbed, especially as we get older. Most of our night calls have been alcoholics and children, not counting the hospital calls. Noose doesn't mind the genuine ones, the sick children or the people who have been vomiting all night and are unable to control their pain. Quite often, those people are happy with advice. Other people get us out of bed for any frivolity.

'Bloody Christ!' Noose muttered one night, beginning an all-too-familiar litany as he fumbled with the bedside light.

'Don't swear!' I murmured sleepily.

'I hope it's not that damn Jones woman, drunk again,' he said. 'Hello!' he barked.

By this time I'd awakened enough to see my life's partner glowering at the telephone. Some other time I might have giggled. Noose with ruffled feathers is quite a sight!

'Uh,' he grunted into the receiver. 'There's nothing I can do until morn–'

I heard a belligerent male voice on the line from across the bed.

'Sir,' Noose said haughtily, 'You'd know better than I if your wife were pregnant.'

To what sounded like the yappings of an unhinged terrier Noose replied patiently, 'It would be far better for you both to come to the surgery in the morning. I'll meet you there at eight.'

By now, we were both awake. I hugged Noose for support and heard the caller say, 'No no, gotta be tonight.'

You can't shift a person who is determined to get you out of bed No Matter What.

Noose slammed down the phone. 'Bastard,' he spat, sliding out of bed and dressing angrily. 'He lives way out the back of beyond and we won't get paid for this.'

'Isn't he the one who comes in panic-stricken, way before the surgery opens, saying that his condom has broken again and he's going to sue the manufacturer?'

'The same,' he said, slamming the door so hard on his way out that the windows clattered.

I switched off the light, hoping to sleep.

Dead quiet overtook the house, as it always does after he storms out, leaving room for the day's ghosts. During the morning a druggie demanded a home visit, which Noose refused. He limped into the surgery in the afternoon claiming to be an epileptic. Yeah right, pull the other one. He *had* to have his drug of choice. Noose refused. Druggie turned belligerent and said why didn't Noose ring his GP in Queensland? Noose told this chap he needed a letter from that GP. He then ducked out to get the town's fire officer, who fixes computers and fortunately happened to be in the office, and coaxed him into the consulting room. They thought they'd have to ring the police but fortunately this druggie left to plague some other poor GP.

I switched on the bedside lamp and tried to read a novel but couldn't concentrate. 3.15: I gave up, switched the lamp off and lay in the dark. 3.28: No way could I get back to sleep. I couldn't when Noose was out, not until I heard the car pull into the garage. 3.46: All sorts of thoughts whizzed along the surface of my mind like a hyperactive helicopter. The roads would be bad on this frosty night; was he driving safely and slowly? Noose wasn't known for his careful motoring habits. 4.03: He wasn't handling stress well; would this be another nail in his coffin? 4.27: I switched the lamp back on and got up to microwave a glass of milk. He'd been gone over an hour. Long ago he'd promised to ring if he'd been away longer than an hour. 4.33: What the hell did they get him out for? I drank my milk huddled over the sink in the kitchen. It was so hot I burned my tongue, which seemed appropriate. 4.38: If he's not home in ten minutes, I'll ring the auto people. This thought comforted me for exactly nine-and-one-half minutes. 4.49: Did he get a puncture? Maybe it wasn't the car, maybe that horrible man bashed him. After all, Noose'd been in a foul mood. Should I call the police?

At 4.55, Noose breezed in and kissed my cheek. I was downstairs making another cup of warm milk. 'That was my shortest, rudest home visit ever,' he said cheerfully, whistling *Old Man River.* Noose had recovered his equilibrium completely. 'The wife lay in bed with nothing wrong whatsoever. Mr Potent just *had* to know. I walked into the bedroom, told them to come to the surgery in the morning, turned around and walked right back out again. I went all that way for absolutely nothing.' Noose grabbed a medical journal from the table and headed up to bed. 'Is there any more of that, my darling wife?' he called over his shoulder.

'Yes, dear,' I said, popping his mug into the microwave and digging out the most banal women's rag I could find from a stack of new magazines.

'Don't know why you read that junk,' Noose said as I carried our drinks to the bedside, magazine tucked under my arm. He'd read it cover-to-cover next morning.

'A simple thank you would suffice,' I replied, putting the glass by his side.

He grimaced.

'What's wrong?' I asked.

'There's too much,' he complained. 'I can't drink all this. I keep telling you–

'Very well, I'll give you less,' I said testily, retrieving the glass and heading to the bathroom to tip some of the liquid into the sink.

'And you know how I feel about waste. You're so extravagant. I keep trying to teach you.'

As I considered whether to throw the glass at him or hit him with the magazine, Noose grabbed the milk and drank it down. 'Ah,' he said, smiling with satisfaction.

I climbed into bed, glowering.

'What's the matter with you? *You* didn't have to go out in the cold.'

Where could I begin? 'No, dear,' I answered, and slithered under the blankets. I turned away from the husband I love more than life itself – I think.

I'm not stupid. I realize that home visits are symptomatic of a deeper problem I doubt I have the courage to face. That night I looked at my husband and reached for the Valium.

Blind faith

Amaranth Fillet

'Awop-bop-a-loo-lop-alop-bam-boo. He's the originator, the innovator,' said Amaranth Fillet. 'Don't look so sceptical. Even someone as straight-looking as I can appreciate the architect of rock-and-roll, Little Richard.' Our headlights unzipped the night, which streamed past the car in endless unfolding ribbons. 'I used to look very different but it put patients off. They didn't trust me. They do now, even though I still feel exactly the way I used to look,' she said. She grinned as the hypnotic path cleared by our headlights impaled possums and wallabies. 'Trust is indispensable in this gig. Sometimes I wonder if my patients wouldn't run naked through the streets if I wrote it on a prescription pad. That engendered trust can be as baneful in a doctor–patient relationship as in a spousal directive.'

THIS OINTMENT SHOULD take care of your sore eye, LC,' I said.

'Thanks, doc,' said the patient across the desk, whose rough and ruddy facial skin made him look like a misshapen football. LC Wickett had what our receptionist described as 'nice legs.' She loved football-shaped calves. Add a football jersey to the shorts LC wore in all weathers and he could have been a boy singer. Some unkind locals said he had the mind of a football. He may've been a slow learner at school, but LC was a fantastic electrician. Everyone I knew used him and didn't mind waiting 'til he was available.

I glanced out the window and saw a bright yellow van parked alongside my battered truck. He'd stencilled *LC Wickett, Electrician* in black on the side, turning the vehicle into an over-sized bumblebee.

I didn't see much of LC. He only came in for minor accidents and prescriptions for infections, like today.

'I'm grateful for your time,' he said, studying the prescription form and nodding slowly.

Not all patients are as uncomplicated as LC Wickett. People want prescriptions for all sorts of reasons. One chap used to plague me, saying that he'd commit suicide unless I gave him drugs. He'd been in and out of jail. He wasn't nasty, just out of sync with the times. If he'd been allowed to wander from village to village playing his tin whistle, having people give him drinks, he'd have been happy. I tried to explain to him the limitations on me as a doctor, but he didn't understand. Eventually he took his own life. Had it happened on my watch, I'd have felt remorseful.

As I didn't see much of the busy electrician, I didn't mind writing him prescriptions. He wasn't the kind of patient who insisted on walking out with one, whether he needed it or not. So many patients aren't happy unless they leave with a script in hand. They don't feel they've got their money's worth – even though many of them don't pay anyway. With antibiotics I tell patients, 'I think you'll be okay. I'll give you a prescription, if you get worse over the next couple of days, get it dispensed.' It locks in beautifully with the logic that demands them but only takes the first three out of the packet. I've taken to giving out more scripts, but fewer are dispensed. It's wisdom borne of desperation, of late-night paybacks.

LC was anything but waspish. After a few people get cranky if you don't give them antibiotics, you start doing so. Gone are the days that Uncle Zoltan was telling me about. Forty years ago the doctor'd pat you on the shoulder and say, 'You'll be right son,' or 'girlie' and out you went. This consumerism is new in medicine and has its risks. One of Uncle Z's patients read the leaflet accompanying her hypertension medication. The possible side effects so appalled her that she decided to be drug-free on her upcoming holiday. She walked around with untreated hypertension for three weeks. If this woman had a stroke, would she have the right to sue the drug company? Chemists get a worse go with these things. The local chemist and I decided to tell patients the same thing: 'It might give you a rash and make you feel dizzy. If you've got any worries just come back and see us.' We've got them covered.

LC Wickett fidgeted. Obviously we'd not yet reached the purpose of his visit.

'Was there something else you wanted to see me about?' I asked.

His face cracked into an embarrassed half-smile. 'Well doc it's me, um, bum.'

'What about it?'

'It itches.'

'Is it worse in the morning or the evening?'

'At night.'

'After you go to bed?'

'That's when I notice it.'

'Doesn't sound like anything to worry about,' I said, writing out a second script without examining LC's nether regions. I usually write multiple prescriptions on one form. For some reason I didn't then.

'Thanks, doc,' he said, visibly relieved. 'I feel better already.'

'Let me know if these don't help.'

Later as I left the surgery for my afternoon off, I noticed one of LC's prescriptions sitting on my desk. He'll need that, I thought. I took it round to the chemist, where I saw the bumblebee van parked in front of the newsagent's next door. I rolled up behind LC and beeped the horn.

'Here, mate,' I said, trotting to his side and waving the prescription, 'this is for your eyes.'

LC looked at the piece of paper for one long, silent minute. Finally a toothy smile radiated from that ruddy face and he said, 'I thought it must be a pretty good cream you got that fixes both me arsehole and me eye.'

We are purposely vague on such prescriptions. I'd written only, *apply to affected area*, which LC Wickett would be sure to do. After all, he trusted me.

Some patients will do anything we tell them whilst others obey their spouses blindly. Ambrose O'Sullivan did as his wife directed. It killed her.

'Divina won't be needing that toe massage now,' I said gently, glancing over my shoulder at the foot of the conjugal bed one frosty winter morning. Joan Baez sang 'Old Blue' from a tape player near the bed.

The big man sighed. 'Aye, but she always used to like it. It's the last thing I can do for her,' he said, reverently releasing the lifeless digit. 'I should have called the ambulance.'

I closed the dead woman's eyes and started to pull the cotton sheet with dainty pink-and-yellow flowers over her head, which the large woman had preferred to bold stripes and practical polyester.

'Not yet, doctor, if you don't mind,' Ambrose said, coming to my side to say his last goodbyes.

We were alone in the room. Ambrose had sent the numerous O'Sullivan children out back to play with the dog. He knelt adoringly by his Divina's deathbed, a sprawling figure with unfinalised features, as if his Maker had got tired or bored and left the job unfinished. Ambrose's nose was broad and flat, barely more than two nostrils. His ears wandered half-heartedly into his head. His eyes held the look I'd seen so many times before in this situation.

'I should have called the ambulance,' he repeated brokenly.

'Your wife stopped you acting, Ambrose,' I said quietly.

Divina had completely dominated her husband. I knew that. Heart disease had plagued Divina for years. I knew that too. Given both factors, should I have counselled Ambrose to ignore her likely protestations and ring for an ambulance in case of trouble?

'Yes, that's right. Look at the trouble I got into when I tried to run the place,' Ambrose said, leaning forward. His eyebrows – short, dark little slashes – descended sharply towards his nose. They stopped halfway back across his brow bone, where his eyes began, forming a triangle. Nothing tight or pinched inhabited Ambrose's face. Even the lines around his mouth meandered from nose to jaw.

Did you ever read *The Secret Life of Walter Mitty*? The protagonist had many guises and schemes, all of them totally hopeless. As a miniature Mitty, Ambrose's judgment and critical faculties were as lost as his physical finesse. Better still to think of him as the dreamer in Lennon's 'Imagine.' In his own way he tried to spread harmony and love, but it smeared more like hardened marmalade with Divina.

One day he decided to rear calves out the back and sell the fatted-up results. He loosed five enthusiastic young heifers in his backyard. That didn't do his garden much good. Not only did they shit all over the place but also their hooves tore up everything. It became a badly run farmyard. Every kid in the district came to pat his calves. The vet then appeared and pronounced ringworm, so Ambrose had to pay for one hundred and twenty children with ringworm. Picture all these kids running around town painted blue! The government condemned and shot every last calf. Ambrose lost his backyard, his calves and his wife's affections. The neighbours didn't see him as a roaring success.

Another time Ambrose ruled as the local chicken king. Day-old chicks were a great seller, because when they finish laying you eat them. Hence the need for new ones. He invested in all the gear and had the things coming out of his ears. Then one day the state government announced that the egg board had a monopoly on the provision of eggs. Anybody who kept more than one chicken had to register and pay a fee. Ambrose's empire disappeared overnight. I've always wondered what he did with his stock, but that's a secret he still guards. The good man went on to a number of other schemes over the years, all of which were complete disasters. His wife finally took over ruling the roost and had henpecked him for the last twenty years.

Divina's domineering nature killed her. She had a coronary in the bedroom. 'Ahh!! I've got terrible indigestion,' she cried, sitting up in bed and clutching her middle.

'I'll get the ambulance, dear,' said Ambrose, heading for the phone. Contrary to appearances he wasn't a total fool. He could recognise a lady having a heart attack.

'No! I've only got indigestion.'

'But Mum–' protested the children, who had all gathered round.

Divina let neither husband nor any of their brood leave her side. The family sat transfixed for two hours, until eventually she keeled over and the spell was broken.

'I should have called the ambulance,' Ambrose said.

'Perhaps she wanted to die at home, Ambrose. It's quite difficult with a very dominant partner,' I replied, hoping to provide some comfort. I didn't add that it takes courage to break that bond of control. It can be very difficult to persuade people they're dying. The wife, often against her better judgment, doesn't call the ambulance in accordance with her husband's wishes. My theory, with which my colleagues may disagree – I know my husband, Wayne, certainly does – is that during a heart attack the heart's output to the brain starts to drop and the oxygen level in the brain falls. The frontal lobe of the brain ceases to function at ninety-five or ninety-six per cent oxygen. It needs that one hundred per cent pure quality stuff in order to change a decision. Consequently, if one decides this is only indigestion, even though it gets worse as the heart output and oxygenation fall, one cannot change that decision. Somebody else has to step in and change it. Ambrose may once have had the courage required to break that bond of control, but his wife wore him down long ago. On the other hand, hypoxia may not have hampered Divina O'Sullivan. She may have known precisely what she was doing and wanted to die at home in her own nest, in her own cotton floral sheets, surrounded by family.

Into the silence around Divina's deathbed burst one of the O'Sullivan children. A large, friendly Labrador lapped at his heels.

'Dad, Blue's in the house!'

Ambrose transferred his hands from wife to canine, which was ecstatic to be inside again after so many years.

'Let him stay, son, if it makes you happy,' Ambrose said with uncontested authority, and smiled sadly. 'We can breed llamas now.'

The night of the bat and the black mamba

Centuria Peale

'Thanks for meeting me here. We're helping to settle in some Somali refugees,' said Centuria Peale. 'I know an empty house isn't very comfortable, but the furniture shouldn't be too far away and neither should the electricity man. Tea?' she asked, vigorously twisting the neck of a Thermos. 'Getting us all settled for the night and the husband off to work the next day was vastly different in Africa than here.' Steam snaked between us as she poured. 'I'm particularly thinking of creatures that glide, slither and ruminate.'

T HANK GOD there were no drums that night. They often went until dawn, sending messages or summonses or Lord knows what. Who did they want and for what? Which of the children would I go to first if the drums heralded a call to war? The ones at this end of the house or the two younger ones? Christy definitely. She wasn't as robust as the others and still had a bout of diarrhoea. What a choice!

I crawled into bed under the mosquito net, my mind a jumble of images. Thank God Yam was home ... The children were finally settled. One sentence buried in an obscure medical book said to give a teaspoon of orange juice if nothing else worked, and Christy kept it down ... What a blessing that Yam relocated us to a medical compound in the city.

Each crank of my mind brought a new thought to the surface. Is there such a thing as a perfect doctor's wife? Many GPs have a passion and a gift for healing. Yam has never minded all the stress and the fuss. He thrives on it. We doctors' spouses can feed the flames or extinguish them. We protect them from intrusion and give lots of tender loving care. Our husbands work very long hours, are always in a rush at lunchtime and often on duty nights and weekends – in fact, *always* on duty. We structured our lives around Yam's work. We still do. Ideally. If I were perfect I would do these things, but I'm not perfect.

In Africa my job was to keep the home fires burning and the children happy. It never bothered me, at least in the early days. That's a good thing or I'd have become very bitter very young. I became a feminist later, after an encounter with the male-dominated church hierarchy. I had daughters by that time and couldn't let them believe that this was acceptable behaviour. But that's another story for another time.

Thank God the drums were silent, or was it a mixed blessing? The sound that replaced them was terrifying. It was a high-pitched squeak and it was right next to my ear. Something had got tangled in the mosquito net between the wall and the bedhead. It was a bat! I screamed as I ran into the hall. I grabbed a broom for some reason and ran out of the house in semi-hysterics without awakening the children – no mean feat.

The scene outside was calm and peaceful. Africans sat in the quadrangle round hurricane lanterns singing hymns and traditional songs. They created a wonderful atmosphere, which unfortunately I was in no mood to appreciate.

'Yam!' I called, starting towards my husband, who was sitting amongst the Africans. Then I stopped a few feet from him. What I saw drove from my mind the flapping and scratching of the horrid creature that had so recently invaded my hair. Into the pool of light slithered a large snake, not just any snake, oh no. This was a black mamba, the most feared snake in Africa, very fast and very lethal. This creature slithered amongst people sitting in little groups on chairs or on the ground, obliviously producing their beautiful music. Nobody noticed it until the thing went into the centre pool of light.

'Snake! Snake!' people cried. 'Kill it! Very very dangerous!'

No one moved, including myself, although a few stones buzzed past our ears.

'Give me that!' Yam cried, grabbing the broom from my hand. He rushed back and hit the black mamba, now quite near the light, with such a tremendous thwack that the broom broke in three pieces, mortally wounding the snake.

Finally one man said, 'You did a dangerous thing.'

'What do you mean?' Yam asked. The lack of visible gratitude offended me. After all, Yam had just saved their lives at great risk to his own.

'When you're near enough to hit him with a stick, you're near enough for a snake to bite you,' the man said.

'What should I have done?' Yam asked curiously.

'You should always kill that sort of snake by throwing big stones at it.' That made sense, as these people were quite good shots with stones. What was dangerous – as we discovered afterwards – was that an African had been busily loading his muzzle-loading shotgun to have a go at it. If he had done so, he could not have avoided hitting somebody.

I insisted that Yam accompany me home after that. I'd had enough for one night.

The next morning was Friday. Yam planned to go off for the weekend to a camp half a day's drive away. He'd loaded up the Land Rover until it was chock-a-block with tents, teaching aids, drugs, food, cooking materials, anything you can imagine. He'd left just room for himself in the driver's seat and one person beside him. Our son begged for a ride to a friend's house. I agreed. I felt like taking a drive. Yam would look after the other children in my short absence. I didn't watch what I was doing as we got into the car. I put the key in the ignition and called out to Christy through the open window to do her homework. I started the engine, put the vehicle in reverse and looked back to see where I was going.

That's when I saw it: a big snake, the colour of a sea otter, curled around the various parts of the steering wheel, with its head poised about ten inches in front of my face, looking straight at me. Nobody knew its name, but all agreed it was poisonous. That doesn't mean anything: they say every snake is *kalisana*.

I put the car into neutral. 'Don't move!' I whispered, reaching sideways across my son with as little movement as possible. I opened the passenger door and said, 'When I give you a shove, I want you to fall out and run as fast as you can,' I whispered fiercely. 'Get your father.' With my terrified son safely out of harm's way, I kicked my door open and slid out sideways, onto my head and shoulders. I did a sorry attempt at a somersault to get away from the vehicle.

Yam came running and helped me to my feet.

'Centy!'

'I'm okay.'

'Really?'

'Yes.'

'Thank God!'

With big, hooked sticks, we pulled out every tent, food box, box of books, everything. We couldn't find the snake. We opened the bonnet. No snake. After combing the car, we wondered if I was imaging the whole thing. The snake couldn't have slithered away unnoticed, because thirty people swarmed the car looking for it. Perhaps it hid somewhere in the car. We didn't find it. A few weeks later, an awful smell in the car got worse and worse. Finally, we located it in the roof. The snake had gone up through a channel alongside the windscreen or the door pillar, and died between the lining of the roof and the roof panel. Why it didn't come out I don't know. Maybe it got stuck.

No one felt like going out after that, so we improvised a family picnic under a nearby baobab tree. Yam hoped to get away early, but we never knew what would walk through the door. As I tried to convince him not to use the Land Rover to go away for the weekend, we saw a group of Africans leading a cow into the compound. They approached the outpatient rooms and the operating theatre. One man had wound a black cloth round him, while the rest wore khaki shorts, T-shirts and singlets.

We had strict rules about bringing cows into hospital grounds. People liked to feed them on the vegetation we tried to grow for shade and to keep down the dust. We treasured every bit of grass we could water – if we had any spare water – and every little tree we could get to grow and bear the shady leaves we craved. Cows ruined trees when they were waist- or shoulder-height. I could see Yam preparing to get quite angry. 'Get this cow out!' he said. 'This is where the patients queue.'

'Ah, well, the cow is the patient,' they said.

'The what?'

'The cow is sick.'

'What's wrong with it?' Yam asked. That was a fatal mistake. He should have said he wasn't a vet.

'It's eaten a piece of a thorn tree, and the thorn tree has gone down into its throat and it can't get it out.'

The poor cow was a black-and-white medium-sized cow with a hump between its shoulder blades. It dripped saliva onto the ground and made vague contortions with its tongue and mouth, as if trying to vomit up something. Two Africans pulled the cow over on its side and sat on it. They twisted its head round so it was vertically upwards. One of them, in an amazing, effortless show of strength, pulled the cow's mouth open with his hand and said, 'It's in there.' They jammed in a stick to hold its mouth open and encouraged Yam to put his hand down to see what he could feel. Yam put his arm down the cow's throat, almost up to his elbow. It was his good arm. I hoped the animal wouldn't bite it off. 'Sure enough I can feel something,' he said. 'It feels like a stick.'

A crowd of nurses and medical people had gathered round. Yam said, 'Quick, go and get me a strong gastrectomy clamp.' One of the nurses ran off. I ran for a camera, to snap my hatless husband in his white shorts, calf-length socks and short-sleeved shirt. The nurse returned shortly with a gastrectomy clamp. Yam managed to ease that down with his other hand. 'Ah,' he said, 'I think I can reach the thorn.' It's very hard to pull your hand out of a cow's mouth, because it's got all these sharp bits on its tongue that point downwards, to make food go down. Yam clamped this thing on the piece of stick and extracted his hand, pulling it with him. Out came a piece of thorn tree about eight-een inches long, with barbarous looking spikes all along it. Everybody, including the cow, heaved a sigh of relief.

'Congratulations, doctor,' people said, and I could see that Yam was rather pleased with himself. He washed all the saliva off his hands.

That was the end of that, or so we thought. Yam's fame as a vet spread fast. After we'd repacked the Land Rover and he'd climbed in to go off for the weekend, a shy man with a big sack approached him. 'What's in the sack?' my husband asked.

'It's the patient.'

It was a sick dog.

'This is the end!' Yam cried. 'The cow was a mistake. The dog would be an even worse mistake. I'm not doing it.'

That was that.

I watched Yam drive away and prayed that the coming night would be free of drums, bats and black mambas, and that the snake in the car had been a hallucination.

I don't know if we'll ever go back.

Mrs McMurtry's dose

Thucydides Hare

*'It was so unexpected,' Professor Thucydides Hare said, cracking
another walnut, which he added to a measuring cup next to a
mound of cooked beetroot. 'Ah-choo! Excuse me.' He tooted into a
square of white linen extracted from his pocket. Any excess weight
in his spidery body went into that nose. It was a life force, a great
pale hook, pocked and winged, which he had wiggled and honked
over the decades to distract suffering children into squeals of
fascinated horror. 'It was my first lesson in medical ethics and
would determine the subsequent course of my career.' From a flurry
of banging cupboard doors Harey emerged with flour, oil, spices,
raisins, currants, vanilla and baking powder. 'That should do it,'
he said. Many childhood visits to the Hares included exuberant
ruddy bread on sallow china, neat rectangles punctuated by
swarthy raisin-and-currant dots and pallid walnut dashes.*

I S THIS PENICILLIN?' She wasn't stupid.
 'Is it because my husband's given me a dose?' asked the
well-dressed woman across the desk.

I'll never forget that day. My answers determined the subsequent course of my medical career. It hadn't occurred to me that
I would confront an ethical dilemma on my very first assignment
with a distinguished gentleman of the old school – the very old
school. Patients don't walk in with signs around their necks saying, *Here's a good one for you, doctor. See if you can sort it out in six
minutes.*

I was feeling particularly contented, for which I make no
excuses other than that I was as green as the grass outside. And I
was off guard, a fatal addition to inexperience and self-satisfac-
tion in a medical setting. Humming jauntily, I peeked into the

waiting room and saw four women. A dark lady in designer knock-offs turned the page of an architectural journal. A sweet motherly type knitted automatically while talking to a female with aggressively grey hair and a grimace. A blond, middle-aged lady in cream silk read a popular feminist tome.

'Mrs,' – I looked down at the file – 'Mrs McMurtry?' I looked hopefully at the maternal knitter, who glanced over at me and smiled.

The silk lady closed her book with a thump and stood up. 'Coming, doctor,' she said.

Maybe she wanted sleeping pills or to renew a prescription. Something non-invasive, I prayed, intimidated by all that elegance. Then I saw a message I'd missed in my haste, a note from the principal attached to the file. *See me immediately,* I read as I followed her down the corridor to the consulting room. After shepherding the lady to a chair opposite the desk, I excused myself and scurried down the hall.

I wasn't humming when I sat down across from my patient a few minutes later. 'Sorry for the interruption, Mrs McMurtry.'

'That's quite all right, doctor,' she said pleasantly, adding, 'This is the third consecutive day I've come.'

'Yes,' I replied, looking at the notes.

Mr McMurtry, a local politician, had brought his wife a little souvenir from a business trip – *gonococci*. At least he had the decency to arrange for her to be treated, but he didn't want her to know why. We gave penicillin then as a single daily injection of long-acting suspension, something like one hundred thousand or two hundred thousand units, over a five-or-seven-day period. We gave it in the buttock, because it was bulky and painful.

'Could you strip down to your undies and hop up on the table? On your tummy, please.'

She looked at me for a long moment, then fired off those two fatal questions: 'Is this penicillin you're giving me and is it because my husband's given me a dose?'

I was an honest chap. She was a patient with a right to know the truth, no matter what my principal said. After all, I had graduated from medical school. I knew something. I wasn't prepared to compromise my beliefs, no matter who issued the commandment.

'Yes, and yes,' I answered earnestly.

All hell broke loose. I never truly understood the meaning of 'to gather oneself up' until that moment. Mrs McMurtry's posture straightened. Her demeanour lost not an ounce of its composure. Her remoteness increased. Heightened facial pallor gave the only indication of the true effect of my words.

'Thank you for your honesty, doctor,' she replied icily.

I prepared the syringes as she slid onto the table.

Poor woman, having to endure such an unpleasant procedure. She submitted with better grace than I could have summoned. She uttered not a word of reproach, nary a whimper during the indignity of being jabbed in the buttocks by a very junior GP wielding syringe after syringe, in an ordeal required by no action of her own.

'Thank you for your honesty, doctor,' she repeated. The quiet way she closed the door as she left did not presage my principal's thundering wrath.

'You did what?!' he screamed after I'd trotted down to see him.

'I, um,' I faltered, the strong staff of truth temporarily wrenched from my quivering knees.

'Go on, explain yourself, if you can,' he spluttered.

I marshalled my forces and squeaked, 'It was the truth.'

'The truth!' he boomed. 'The truth!' I was petrified. 'You have ruined a marriage and lost the practice not one valuable patient but an entire family – not to mention the unhappiness your honesty' – he spat the word – 'will bring to all concerned, including yourself.'

I thought about my new wife and our idealistic promises to each other. 'Surely telling the truth cannot be such a hideous thing,' I replied resentfully.

This was before the days of the women's liberation movement. Concepts like truth-telling belong to a later era. At that time, medical ethics as we understand it did not exist in our intensely paternalist profession. The doctor was a god. Patients didn't question his – usually his – decisions and actions, so Mrs McMurtry's inquiries were unexpected and unsettling. I blurted out the truth without thinking. And if I had stopped to reflect?

'You have destroyed that marriage,' he repeated.

'Why didn't you see her yourself, then?'

'Because, dear sir,' he replied slowly, 'I thought your level of ability sufficiently developed to conduct such a session, an opinion unfortunately not validated.'

I hung my head. Telling the truth now seemed like a selfish act.

'You will be informed at the end of the day if your further services are required. I rather doubt it.'

A much-deflated locum saw a few more patients. The afternoon wore on. I had just finished writing a script when the phone rang. 'This is it,' I thought glumly. 'On the job a day and a half and already I've ruined the lives of two adults and God knows how many children. Multiply that over a career.'

The telephone's insistence interrupted my calculations. 'Yes?' I said.

I recognised the responding grunt. At least, after today I would never see my principal again, to my eternal relief and certainly his.

'I have decided to keep you on due to prior commitments to my family, commitments that I would break if I could. Unfortunately I have exhausted my store of spousal good will, although why I am explaining this to you I do not know.'

I breathed a silent sigh of relief.

'Please,' he said, 'I beg of you, do not make any more heroic decisions. Just refer patients to me. I will be back in exactly twelve days. If there is an emergency or if you have any problems whatsoever, even small ones, please, *please*, consult my good colleague down the road. The receptionist knows how to reach him, and I have been on the phone with him this afternoon.'

I detected a note of desperation in his voice. 'You put me in this position,' I replied, with no good humour.

'An error of judgment for which I shall pay for the rest of my days. This is a small place, you know.'

How should I have handled Mrs McMurtry's questions? I replay a variation of my response in my head, with the benefit of many years' experience. I should have called in both husband and wife and sat them down next to one another, with myself nearby, not across the desk, my knees almost touching theirs. I should have said to Mr McMurtry, 'If you want to save your marriage, you must confess to your wife and beg her forgiveness.' I should have taken Mrs McMurtry's hand and told her that everyone makes mistakes. From there, my own good sense and experience would have guided me.

By avoiding the truth, she might have steered her marriage to calm waters, despite being mated to a cigar-smoking, loud-mouthed, gonorrhoea-ridden bully. The principal knew about her floundering marriage. He had the greater knowledge and experience.

On the other hand, my principal and Mr McMurtry were golfing partners. They colluded to keep the politician's wife in the dark, when she had every right to know what ailed her.

Mrs McMurtry taught me my first lesson in medical ethics.

To this day, the poor woman visits me whenever the option of telling the brutal truth to a patient confronts me. One thing I was spared, thank God: I never employed an inexperienced locum with a different practice philosophy, who was presented with a truth-telling dilemma.

Saying it not-so-straight

Zoltan Nagy

*'Yes pet, that is entirely correct, Zoltan Nagy is pensive tonight,'
said the good doctor. 'Must be the Southern weather getting up
my nose. I cannot get away from all this moisture, entering and
leaving my body, mint julep and lemonade, perspiration and
urine, never-endingly accompanied by somebody vocalising or
blowing a horn. I am floating in a world of voodoo and vice. This
city has another life, I can feel it in my waters, a life of interment
and crypts, subterfuge and stealth. You know, my dear, that we
GPs live in a world of secrets, secrets that save, secrets that kill,
patients' secrets and our own, both professional and private.
Concealment can lead to mistakes or worse, far worse.'*

I HAVE A RASH on my lower leg, doctor,' said twenty-year-
old Jacqueline in Wednesday evening surgery late one rainy
night.

I had not a clue that she would become the classic example of a
patient withholding crucial information that surfaced afterwards.

I examined her. 'You have a heart murmur, you know. Maybe
from your rheumatic fever.' In those days, the prevalence of
rheumatic hearts made subacute bacterial endocarditis, or
inflammation of the inside of the heart from infection, more
common than it is now. 'How do you feel?' I asked.

'Perfectly well, doctor. I'm just checking,' she said.

'I will take some blood. Come in Friday for the results.'

That Friday her rash had disappeared, her blood tests did
not show anything and her heart sounded the same. Again she
assured me she felt perfectly well. I was unhappy despite her
assurances, because bacterial endocarditis makes you feel
awful.

That night she died. Her heart valve failed. One side of her heart pumped blood into her lung, but the other side did not pump it out. Fluid filled her lungs and she died rapidly.

Every doctor makes wrong diagnoses. As an intern in accident and emergency, I missed meningitis in an infant. I had been working fifty-five hours straight when a young woman brought in her baby. I gave her a prescription and said to bring it back the next day if it was not better. She did, and the baby was much worse. I recognised meningitis immediately. I never had the courage to follow up to see if the baby died or suffered permanent brain damage.

For every genuine mistake, there are ten imagined. Luckily, I have never been sued. Those of my colleagues who have been are often excellent doctors, shattered by this affront to their caring – often carried out in a grossly discourteous way. Occasionally doctors ask for it by behaving badly. Patients can be just as naughty – understandable, of course, when they are sick.

Something else is understandable: a certain brusqueness at three in the morning. My colleagues and I rocket from deep sleep to hyper-alertness, but at what psychic cost? Can we obtain and retain vital information? I hope and intend that whatever I do is the best of which I am capable, but I cannot work miracles with inadequate information. I am not a mind reader. Often facts come out afterwards about which I knew nothing, as with Jacqueline.

The coroner's officer rang the morning after Jacqueline died. 'You saw her on Friday. You can write a death certificate, can't you, doctor?' he asked. I thought, No, Zoltan Nagy, you do not bury your mistakes. They did a post-mortem and found what had happened. As I had suspected, fragments of the heart valve caused the rash by breaking off and pushing out to the skin surface in the small blood vessels.

I was very upset. I do not like losing twenty-year-olds. Her family were equally upset and wanted to sue me. Today I would probably be in litigation up to my eyeballs. I suggested using the Medical Council. They would be as tough on me as any court and there would be a case in law if they found against me. If not, the family could still have a case in law. This way cost nothing. The family were not rich so that is what we did. In fact the Council found that I had done everything possible. I still did not like it!

The mother rang to abuse me every Friday night for years. It did not worry me terribly much as it was good therapy for her. I listened at first, but in the end held the phone at arm's length and carried on reading my journals. When she ran out of breath I said, 'Yes, I am sorry. These things happen. I would love to know what happened.' Eventually she stopped ringing and I put it in the back of my mind.

Eighteen years later a lady asked me during a consultation, 'Do you remember Jacqueline?'

'I am not likely to forget her!'

'Do you know what happened?'

'Yes, she died.'

'Nothing to do with you,' the patient said gravely. 'We were both typists in the same firm. Jacqueline told me that she'd been to see you but hadn't told you how awful she felt. She knew you'd put her in hospital. "It's my twenty-first birthday party tomorrow," she told me. She'd been looking forward to it all year. "I'll see the doctor Monday and tell him how I really feel."'

It took eighteen years to find out I was right and she was right, we were both right but we did not swap the information. She took a gamble and lost. In fact she would have died anyway. Technology was not good enough to save her. Her heart would have collapsed. Maybe with a cardiac surgeon available in hospital, we could have put her on a pump quickly enough. She was so far gone that even today it would have been touch and go.

The retrospectoscope, an instrument much beloved by lawyers and gossips, proved me right in my suspicions but wrong in my lack of perseverance. I did not connect the consultation date, date of birth and significance of the twenty-first birthday. I am still sorry for the mother, who had died by the time I found out the cause of death. It would have eased her pain. She was set in her ways so she might not have believed me. She needed to make that phone call every Friday and I took it. Would I have time today to take such calls? I hope so, despite all the blasted paperwork the government throws my way. I would prefer to listen to that poor woman's abuse than the bleatings of some idiot wielding a pen.

~ ∾ ~

Perhaps it is better for some secrets to remain corked. Once the genie is out of the bottle it is difficult to stuff it back in. My second reminiscence concerns a cluster of patients and knowing when to back off. Ferreting out the hidden may do more harm than good. Consider the context and the levels of tension and anxiety. Do not try to do too much too fast. Many husbands deceive their wives for years. Wives deceive their husbands as well. It is a dance around the edges, all dark hints and furrowed brows. People go through their lives protecting their secrets. I certainly have mine. A private life is a good thing.

The longer I am in this business, the more firmly I believe that it is deluded to expect spouses to be all things to each other. We medicos know this well, as do psychologists, police and divorce lawyers. Secrets are part of the fabric of communication. Does a middle-aged woman past menopause and minus a sex drive, with grown children and grandchildren, really want to know about her husband's sexual peccadilloes? He is as driven by his hormones as she is by hers. Does an uxorious elderly husband need to know that his beloved wife of half a century has been meeting her first lover clandestinely for the last forty years?

The role of a doctor is not always to extract the maximum number of verbal or nonverbal facts from a patient. As in those ancient Japanese paintings, what is unrevealed is respected and not pursued into submission. We do not always know why people come to us. They give us an edited version. They may be searching, to see if they like us, if we are sympathetic enough and willing to listen to this or that particular problem or to summon up the courage to bare their souls.

Shortly after the Masters and Johnson book appeared in the 1960s, I discovered that bringing up sexual matters lost you patients. Without care they told you too much. They went home and thought, 'I didn't tell him *that*, did I? Ohhhh, I can never face him again.' That was that. You lost a family. You have got to stop people before they reach the full flow and ask them if they really want to discuss it. This may be difficult: the range of human sexual behaviour is enormous. Anything you can think of people have done, although they are not always game to discuss it.

Many patients do not want to discuss the past, especially if it includes suffering and sorrow. With Iris and Lavender, two part-Aboriginal sisters, I ferreted out information I thought vital for their health. With Old P and Mr Ward, two returned servicemen, I did not. Home visits would have been most useful in all these cases, but they never called me out.

Iris and Lavender refused to talk about their pasts, and pasts they certainly had. They had produced twenty-eight children between them, most of whom they lost, and not through death. Women's refuges came in after the Pill decimated the number of children women bore. If refuges had existed, I doubt they could have coped with Iris, Lavender and their trail of children. Far easier to toss out a man than to orchestrate thirty pairs of feet crossing the domestic threshold into freedom. Women were at the mercy of their mates. They got thumped if he was a bastard. They stayed in line, bore more children and eventually took to drinking themselves. The last two or three children were often foetal alcohol syndrome babies, with the older ones in better nick. The younger ones were thin, with small heads and elfin, peaked faces coming to a point. They were quite distinctive and also less intelligent. You still see these people around occasionally, but the birth rate has been falling since 1963.

Iris and Lavender were forerunners of women's liberation. If they did not like a man or the way he treated them, out he went. They did exactly as they pleased, which included spending most of their time manless. Quite a feat, considering the number of children underfoot.

The sisters had not only pasts but also presents. I cobbled together their histories through a network of colleagues and friends – no mean feat, let me tell you. I remember one particular accident and emergency ward. Oh Iris of the many skull X-rays! Oh Lavender of the many tetanus injections! I can still hear the casualty resident.

'Oh God, not again!' said that harassed individual, looking down with resignation at the large woman with the slack abdomen lying on the examining table. 'She's got a skull injury and cuts on the head,' he said, repeating a familiar litany. 'Skull X-ray,' he ordered automatically.

One of Iris's happy pastimes included pot fights in pubs. She regularly got herself beaten senseless. The resident and I gave up trying to obtain a proper medical history. Iris's story changed every time. Nobody had ever counted Iris's skull X-rays until I researched the subject many years later and found she had had three hundred during this ten- to fifteen-year period. They were not done routinely in those days, only on head injuries.

Getting cut was her sister's favourite thing. Lavender got stabbed or into fights with bottles or fell on glass with tedious regularity. Accident and emergency sewed her up. Had she had an anti-tetanus injection? Lavender never knew, being drunk. Nobody ever checked the notes. As she was not a pleasant character, somebody invariably said, 'Give her one, sister' and got her out of the place as quickly as possible.

Some patients do not obfuscate their pasts, they simply do not wish to discuss them. This is what worries me about post-traumatic stress disorder. It may be dangerous to disinter what is buried in the back of somebody's mind. Can you repack the genie once you have released it? My returned servicemen fall neatly into two groups: those who tried to manipulate the system and probably never went overseas and those who had been overseas and shot at. The former aired it *ad nauseam*. They end up over-investigated and over-treated and never any the better for it, like poor Mr Ward. He comes in every week with a new crisis, at great inconvenience to everybody. He can't drive due to his 'spells' and has a mechanically challenged wife, so the local community sister constantly rearranges her schedule to bring him to the surgery. Our receptionist patiently double-books Mr Ward at the

SECRETS FROM THE BLACK BAG

last minute. We do not always remember to inform relief receptionists to double-book Mr Ward, which results in some disagreeable confrontations. He exhibits the classic symptoms: persistent startle response changing into an angry-hostile outburst, repetitive battle dreams – which I question – and irritability and tremors.

I can tell instantly which members of the two groups fare better in daily life, before they get from the waiting room to the consulting room. Mr Ward leans on his wife, literally depends upon her for every step he takes. She invariably looks overwhelmed, her square shoulders drooping a little more each time I see them. Poor woman. What began as movies and moonlight ended as old tapes and a nightlight. For better or for worse indeed. As he struggles towards the consulting room, Mr Ward looks twenty years older than his age, beaten and bent. His guilt and the blurring passage of time conspire to give him war wounds, a deception in which I collude.

The latter group are a different kettle of fish altogether. They do not talk about their war experiences and I do not ask. Old P chugs into the consulting room under his own steam, a cargo train nowhere near the end of its long haul. Post-traumatic stress manifests differently in Old P. What a wonderfully capable, decent, hard-working chap! One day, Old P came in with a dreadful gash across his forehead. He'd run into a door in the middle of the night after a nightmare about Borneo. 'The government brain-washed us, doc, and I fell for it,' he said. All my World War II veterans have in common their intense hatred of the Japanese. Old P was no exception, partly because of what war forced him to do. Tears ran down his cheeks as I stitched him up. 'The Japs used to grin when we shot them. We aimed for their front teeth, right here in the middle. Teeth flew everywhere when we pulled the trigger.' That knock on the head started Old P talking about the war. I always let him initiate it. He is the only one among the latter group who does. Perhaps the others will as they become disinhibited with age, and as those faraway war memories displace more recent ones.

The badly wounded ones show fewer emotional problems. Note this inverse relationship. Serious physical wounds satisfy a punitive need of survivor guilt, of what we used to call Buddy Guilt or Unit-Guilt Reaction. Old P came back but his mates did not. He paid for it, in his own mind. I do not think anyone will ever know the truth about Mr Ward, as his war records are inconclusive. It's probable he did not go to the front. If he did, he was either not wounded or only slightly injured. Mr Ward remains unresponsive – resistant – to any suggestion of psychotherapy.

Conflict exists between fear and the urge to flee, and duty and the need to fight. Which of my two old soldiers did repeated exposure to trauma deplete more? Which did the war make more fatigued, disillusioned, and vulnerable? *That* genie remains firmly in the bottle. Maybe we should air it. It never worked with Iris and Lavender, survivors of a different kind of war. In the meantime, my veterans and I grow old together silently, apparently without any great harm to anybody.

Secrets serve an adaptive function. I advise young medicos to create an appropriate emotional climate before plunging in. Someone will pay the price for secrets, concealed or revealed.

Unheard cris du coeur

E Manley Dew

The world had greyed, not the wet-rain grey that makes colours throb but the dry hushed pearl of twilight. 'Out of the big three – love, family and career – life gave me one. Well, one-and-a-half,' said E Manley Dew. From the top of her pack she lifted an old photograph, enlarged and grainy, of a young man grinning at the camera. She cradled it with two hands, a sacred offering. The girl who wept over a casket had become a serene and trusted caregiver but, as they say locally, still waters run deep and you never know.

M R BEAUMONT,' I called, rapping at the rotting wooden door. The wood absorbed my knock, so I stepped inside. The dark cottage smelled of old man living alone: urine, dirty dishes and clothes, stale food, wood fire and cigarette smoke. Something was missing: flat beer.

I'd been in a particularly good mood that day during morning surgery. The drive in had been pleasant. **Wattlebirds** squawked and the colours of the year shifted overnight from green and blue to yellow and brown. I'd not had to tell any patients they were terminally ill; indeed, some of my favourites had been in for relatively trivial ailments. The last thing I expected was attention-seeking behaviour from a crusty old man.

June rang through. Best receptionist we've ever had: discreet, taciturn, knew everybody and all their nicknames and married names. Never once let the patients trick her into divulging private information. Bit of an old tyrant. Ran the office. Ran me. We're still living with her redecoration of the waiting room. Vomit-pink with lilac-and-lime trim. Watercolours of anonymous beaches surround a print of a snowy peak that Dad's predecessor left.

'It's Mr Beaumont, doctor,' she said.

'Who?'

'William Beaumont, your father's patient. He just got out of hospital yesterday. Says he's collapsed,' she said, raising her eyebrows ever so slightly. 'He asked for you.'

I dropped everything, leaving June to sort out the full waiting room.

In that dark cottage, Mr Beaumont lay face down on the floor, not far from the door. He'd seen eighty summers and grown hairy as a goat. Poor old chap. He must have been trying to go for help when he collapsed. A thousand thoughts crowded my mind in a split second, most of them concerning the plight of the elderly forced to live alone and decisions I'd be making. I went to turn him over. Mr Beaumont opened his eyes, looked up and winked.

I didn't move. I couldn't.

He rolled over, sat up and said with a nasty grin on his face, 'That'll teach you.'

I was too shocked to speak.

Mr Beaumont lived forty minutes' drive away, through some of the loveliest countryside I've seen, but I'm partial to verdant rolling hills studded with black-and-white cows.

Mr Beaumont was playing doggo, pretending to be unconscious. 'You bloody well think you're so great. Well I've got news for you, love. I'm just as smart as you.'

'Mr Beaumont, I don't even know you.'

'You would say that.'

'Look, Mr Beaumont, I've never met you before. I've just left a lot of sick patients and driven for forty minutes to come here.'

He laughed unpleasantly. 'I showed you then, didn't I?'

'I have to go now.'

'You ignored me in hospital yesterday. Bloody doctors.'

'I have no idea who you are.'

'Liar,' Mr Beaumont snarled, baring his horrid teeth at me.

'What do you mean?'

'Your father's my doc, and I know you doctors talk about us patients. I saw youse talking about me in hospital.'

'Just because you're my father's patient doesn't mean I know you or that my father talks about you, Mr Beaumont. Think about it.'

'You ignored me. Bloody stuck-up bitch.'

It was horrible. I had had enough. 'Mr Beaumont, I never want to have anything to do with you ever again.' I've never said that to a patient before or since.

Later, Dad filled me in. Billy Goat Beaumont had retired to the town shortly after our arrival. No one knew why. He worked in sawmills his entire life, turning forest red gums into railway sleepers and street-paving blocks for faraway places like Melbourne and London. Mr Beaumont was a fanatic teetotaller. Dad never found out why, until one day Mr Beaumont told him in a weak moment. Dad said it taught him something about being inquisitive with patients. Mr Beaumont changed after his confession, becoming distant. Dad felt the confession damaged the relationship permanently and berated himself for asking in the first place. Apparently Mr Beaumont had got drunk only once in his life, as a teenager, part of some rite of passage. His friends goaded him to taste the pleasures of black velvet, that nasty habit of raping Aboriginal girls. Next day, his actions so horrified Mr Beaumont that he vowed never to touch another drop. Dad suspects he also enforced upon himself the penance of a celibate life, or at least an unmarried one. Dad was never able to guide the relationship back to where it had been before, and it always bothered him.

I told Mr Beaumont that I didn't want to see him again. I never did. He got what he wanted, or needed, from me. He got my attention, but I couldn't give him acceptance. I'm sorry about that. He's dead now. Patients' *cris du coeur* take many forms. Maybe I should have handled Mr Beaumont differently, but he made me angry.

Mrs Dove never called me out frivolously, so I knew something was seriously wrong that summer morning. I took the call in the tearoom out the back, where we were having an early feed on ginger biscuits.

'I ache all over, doctor. Maybe if you could just, on your way home—'

'I'll pop round at lunchtime,' I replied.

'Better get over there straight away,' June commanded. I was beholden to her and she knew it. She knew everything about me, in fact. During my teenage years of boy troubles, she always scooted me in to see Dad before the other patients – a family emergency, she explained to the querulous in a tone no one dared question. To that loyal soul, a family emergency was far more important than Mrs Brown's tablets or Mr Nicholson's funny turns.

'I'm on my way,' I replied, brushing crumbs from the corner of my mouth.

Mrs Dove was one of those very white old ladies: snow-white frizzy hair, creamy skin, translucent hands, pale blue eyes. She was in bed when I arrived, paler than usual.

'What's the problem, Mrs Dove?'

'I feel like I'm dying, doctor.'

'Can you be more specific?'

'My right shoulder hurts, and all my joints are stiff.'

As I moved to examine Mrs Dove, I saw a photograph tucked up on top of the wooden dresser.

'Is that you as a young woman?' I asked, stretching for the yellowed photo.

'No, doctor,' she replied. 'That's Mrs Millerup. An automobile accident got her. She donated her kidneys to my late husband. Gave him an extra sixteen-and-a-half years, Mrs Millerup did.'

'I see.'

'I wish he were here with us now. I look at that photograph every day and thank God for Mrs Millerup. Convinced me to become an organ donor, not that anyone would want these old bones and body parts, although maybe they will when you're done with me, dear,' Mrs Dove said, goodness beaming forth. 'I wish I could offer you a cup of tea.'

'Never you mind about that, Mrs Dove,' I said. 'I'll just take some blood to confirm my diagnosis, but I'm sure you have polymyalgia.'

As Mrs Dove rolled up the sleeve of her nightdress, two photographs slipped to the floor from underneath her pillow. I picked them up and handed them back, glancing at them casually, my mind preoccupied with arranging a laboratory courier for Mrs Dove's blood. Plastic frames protected those tattered headshots of bygone days. Mrs Dove's pension didn't run to more elaborate protection of her memories.

'Mr Dove as a young man,' she said of one photograph. The other she pushed beneath her pillow. 'I didn't marry until I was thirty-five. I didn't want to be alone anymore, doctor, and I didn't have anyone to care for, not like you, so I married Mr Dove. He was a good husband and a good companion, but there was no spark, at least on my part,' she said, sighing. 'Doctor, since Mr Dove and I tied the knot, I've been observing marriages. Of course, my experience is extremely limited, but I have noticed a few things.'

'Such as?'

'These days, people put love and marriage in the same category as smelling roses or being pricked by thorns or any other sensation. They say it's not right unless you feel it in your bones. Well, I feel the cold in my bones but I don't want to marry it.'

'So many kinds of love exist,' I agreed, trawling my own mental photographs.

'There was that unlikely match at the church choir.'

'I remember,' I said, patting Mrs Dove's hand. 'The choir master and the soprano.'

'No one thought it would last, but it has. A spiritual basis is just as relevant as a bone feeling. And what about a meeting of the minds?'

'What's that second photo, the one under the pillow?' I asked.

'It shouldn't be there. I know that doctor, but I thought I was dying.'

'Tell me about it.'

She pulled it out gently, with the force of fifty years' love. 'He was the love of my life.'

'He looks familiar,' I said, straining to place the face.

'I grieved for that man half of my life,' Mrs Dove said, eyes filling at the old hurt. 'William and I got engaged at a young age. It was a love match, very much so, and our parents approved. He was so charming and cheerful. Then the day after his stag party he just disappeared,' she recalled, silent tears streaming, 'which I do not wish to discuss.'

'I'm sure I've seen that face before.'

'I ran into William again, near the end of his life. Someone told me he had moved to the area, to a shack up the bush. I tried to see him.'

'What was William's surname?' I asked, a light dawning.

'Beaumont,' she replied reluctantly, gazing at the photo with sublime love.

'Mr Beaumont!' I exclaimed, dropping the pen I was using for the pathology form.

'My William,' Mrs Dove said softly.

'What happened when you went out to see him?'

'He wouldn't let me in, doctor. I heard he called you not long afterwards.'

I left to return to work. The lab confirmed my suspicions that afternoon about Mrs Dove's condition. Polymyalgia is a great condition to treat. Patients feel lousy with it. You give them Prednisolone and they feel fantastic. Mrs Dove was no exception.

'I'm going to give you some tablets,' I rang to tell her just before leaving for the day. 'They should fix you right up. Let me know if they don't.'

The following week, June brought in a letter from Mrs Dove. 'I know a lot of people knock doctors and say you're late all the time,' it read, 'but it was so lovely of Doctor to come and visit. I felt terrible. Those tablets she gave me made me feel lovely.'

There are few conditions in medicine we treat with such dramatic results. Polymyalgia is one, as Mrs Violet Dove can attest. As for hearing the cry of a patient in a different kind of pain, sometimes that's not so easy.

Family networks

Dexter Veriform

*'Often we'd find a sack of potatoes in the boot of the car, a
haunch of venison by the back door or a freshly caught trout
delivered shyly during the season,' said Dexter Veriform. 'These
days the mind returns to my years in a corner of Scotland where
nobody ever really died. The oldies telescoped centuries when
speaking of their grandparents. I felt closer to the nineteenth
century than to this one. That place was big on kinship. So many
kinds of families. I tried so hard to give my patients what they
asked for or what I thought they needed. Now this,' he whispered,
spreading his hands in a jerky arc encompassing the visitors'
room at his prison.*

WEE DONNIE MACKAY had a certain charm, until he
took to drink and became psychotic. He wasn't fit to
own a gun. Great shame. Now, I've never liked guns
or been a shooter or a hunter, but I realise why people have to
have them.

Donnie MacKay lived with his parents in a cottage that
belonged to an old Highland estate. His father worked on the
grounds, his mother in the big house. At thirty-five, Wee Donnie
was completely ignorant of the ways of the world, but he was
good at his job. Chopping up firewood was like snapping match-
sticks for him.

I was at home one night when the local policeman rang up.
That was in the days before the change in my relationship with
the representatives of law and order.

'It's Wee Donnie MacKay, doctor.'

'What's happened?'

'He's taken drink, a lot of it,' came the reply.

'And?'

'He's up here with a gun and we feel that since you know the family very well you might have some luck.'

'I'll be right up.'

When I got there, I found that Donnie had gone psychotic on spirits. He was holding the forces of law and order at bay.

It was like a film, with everybody gathered around at a safe distance, including his mother and father, with the villain inside. He'd broken every window and now defied anyone to come near him.

'I've got a loud hailer here if you want to use it, doc,' offered the policeman.

I took the megaphone. 'It's the doctor, Donnie,' I yelled, my mouth against the cold metal. My shouting startled everybody and nearly blew the house down.

'You don't have to yell, doc,' the policeman said. 'Just speak normally.'

'It's the doctor, Donnie,' I repeated, modifying my tone. 'What do you think you're doin', mon? You're frightening everybody.'

'They've frightened me and they've done things that I don't approve of,' Donnie shouted.

I wasn't sure what to do next.

'If you come a bit closer, I'll tell you,' said Donnie.

'You won't shoot me, will you?' I asked.

'Ohhhh, I wouldna shoot you, doc, not 'til heaven freezes on earth.' Donnie combined a religious upbringing with a simple mind. No one found his sayings blasphemous because people knew he meant well.

I walked forward, holding my bag in front of me just in case.

He opened the door. A great strapping fellow with thick red curly hair and a florid, freckly face confronted me. Wee Donnie wore an intensely bright turquoise shirt.

'What on airth are you doing, mon?' I asked. I found myself slipping into the local dialect, something I rarely did and would try not to do again. 'You're causing a lot of trouble.'

'I'm getting my own back on them, doc. Come in.'

I went in.

'Somebody's been writing letters to my parents about me accusing me of things,' he said, distressed.

'What things?'

'Hell's manna, doc! They're no true.'

'Do you know who it is?'

'Aye.'

'Well who is it, mon?'

'It's a girrrl, accusing me of all sorts of things.' He showed me the letters.

'You know these things aren't true, so why make all this fuss about it?'

'It upsets Mum and Dad.'

'You know that's not a good reason, really, to do this.'

'She's a bit nutty herself.'

'She's nuts about you,' I said, perusing a letter.

'I'm not the marryin' sort, doc,' Donnie said, shaking his head vehemently. 'When marriage happens, heaven and high water stink.'

'It's not *that* bad, mon. A lot of people do it.'

'Aye, and a lot of people are miserable. I've got eyes. If I married her, all hell would have to pay. And who would take care of Mum?'

That was my opening. 'You won't be able to take care of your mother if the police take you off to jail for hurting someone with that gun, Donnie.'

That was the end of that. It was a very short house call indeed, with no diagnosis to be made. I was petrified, I'll tell you! I got hold of the gun and walked out with Wee Donnie.

Donnie couldn't get his gun license renewed. A few years later, the letter-writing girl finally wore him down. They married and now have a houseful of healthy bairns and Donnie's no worse for it. The heavens haven't parted, nor have the hells.

~ ∞ ~

Now, nobody ever disappears up there, in Wee Donnie's part of the world. People may leave physically or die, but the tide of talk deposits their stories in the sea of local mythology. I practised for my first eighteen months out of medical school in that area and still go up when I can. Over time I've come to know these people very well. Their family networks have helped me to reflect on each patient's place and situation within those systems as well as within the wider community.

Wee Donnie had a cousin who married well. Mrs Reid pursued artistic interests and dabbled in photography before marriage. Her daughter, Maggie, Donnie's niece, had multiple sclerosis. I'd treated Maggie for influenza during my first locum, so we were well acquainted before she contracted the disease. Maggie taught me about courage in the face of adversity, a different sort of courage than the forester's bewildered variety. Multiple sclerosis clusters near the north and south poles, in the higher latitudes. We still don't know what causes it. I've found great satisfaction in looking after people with such illnesses over a long period of years. A bit of me dies when they die.

Maggie Reid did not die. She was one of my success stories, although I didn't know what the outcome would be that dreary spring day long ago when Mrs Reid first called me out. Maggie was a lovely lass of fifteen years. I remember her voice to this day, a sweet sound like the tinkling of birch leaves fluttering on a spring breeze. How it contrasted with her big, ungainly body. Maggie obviously took after her father, because her mother was a sprig of a thing. They lived with Maggie's brother and sister on one of the big properties, in a large grey house overlooking the loch whose massive windows revealed the water's changing moods. Maggie's paternal grandfather had built the solid stone house between the wars.

That day, I passed over a cattle grid through the open wrought iron gate. What's Maggie doing home during the school term, I wondered as I watched several gardeners working magic on the great lawn sloping to a ha-ha.

Soon I sat next to Maggie's bed. She looked upset. So did her mother. 'What's the matter, Maggie?' I asked.

Mother answered before daughter could speak. 'Maggie was sent home from boarding school in Edinburgh because she would not behave herself.'

'This is not the Maggie I know,' I said.

'They just couldn't cope with her.'

'I wasn't naughty,' Maggie protested, nervously twirling her long, dark hair around a forefinger.

'What do you call it, then?' Mrs Reid demanded. 'You're just like your father.' Mr Reid, a lawyer, had departed several years earlier to marry a famous film star.

'Maggie, what's the matter?' I asked gently.

'I keep on getting giddy and dizzy, doctor, and I can't see the blackboard.'

'Did nobody at your school ever think of taking you to the doctor to see if something was wrong?'

'No, doctor,' Maggie said, hesitating.

'Go on.'

'Um, they sent me home for being naughty when, um–' the poor lass stumbled.

'When she wet the bed,' Mrs Reid finished.

'They really lost their temper with me,' Maggie said belligerently, using a tone she saved for grown-ups.

By this time, I was certain of the diagnosis, even though the various ways that multiple sclerosis presents are legion. 'I want you to see Mr Stoward,' I said. 'He's a neurologist in Glasgow. I'll make the appointment for you.'

'I'm not going to see anyone.'

'I'll go with you, Maggie,' I said.

'What's wrong with me, doctor?'

Poor Maggie. Mr Stoward confirmed that she had multiple sclerosis. It was more difficult to treat back then, with fewer wheelchairs and less public tolerance. Mr Stoward recommended a course of daily injections of ACTH, a hormone that stimulates the body's own supply of cortisone.

Every day for twelve months, I travelled the eight miles along a single-track road by the loch to give the young lady her injections, which the government supplied. People don't realise the commitment you have to make. There were house calls during the day as well and one had to do them. You couldn't *not* go because your family or friends had made other plans. People were very respectful then and did not call me out frivolously.

One Saturday morning during that year, my son came along to show Maggie our two cocker spaniel pups. She loved animals. As always, we went to the back door at eight o'clock in the morning. There was no view round the back, only the offices and kitchen. The family had made a bedroom for Maggie downstairs in a small room with a wood floor near the loo. They'd furnished it nicely, with Oriental carpets, books, a television and photographs of pop singers. There was no central heating, so the place was freezing in winter.

I gave Maggie her injection and we had our usual chat. No one had believed she was ill and suddenly she was receiving daily injections.

'Still feeling seasick all the time?' I asked.

'Yes, doctor.' There was no spark to her at all.

'I've brought along someone today, Maggie. He wants to show you something.'

Maggie's sad countenance brightened considerably at the sight of those pups. She inquired about them often after that.

Dramatically, Maggie improved, as multiple sclerosis patients do. Then she got bad again. Maggie and I are growing old together. She's had two children and two husbands and now gets about on a supporting frame. I keep in touch with Maggie through Donnie whenever I go back. During my last visit, Maggie was up from London. We spoke on the telephone. She's got a funny way of talking, because of her disease. No more tinkling birch leaves. And Donnie's as happy as ever and keeps off the grog, as far as I can tell.

Following orders

Tommy MacDonald

*'Yes and no,' said the man marooned in self-sufficiency. Women
looking for a peg of need had a hard time hooking on. The night
oozed around us, molasses-dark. Sticky ferns left cold wet
imprints on my black spandex pants. Tommy MacDonald leaned
away from the fire, a Wild West cowboy born one hundred years
too late. He was rumoured to be slow on the draw, to the delight
of his women. He laughed a great unapologetic whoop. 'Yes, I
need to feel the wind on my face. No, it's not always easy. Three
tales come to mind,' he said, fair hair flat against his skull like
Jesse James's, eyebrows straight and narrow as Wyatt Earp's.*

SQUARE PEGS IN round holes, one ex-wife says. You can't
force some things no matter how hard you try, says
another. They may analyse me to their hearts' content but
it's simple. I'm a wanderer, I never perch long, it's not in my
nature. I'm a throwback to a great-grandfather who died drunk
on horseback in the bush after a life of managing banana planta-
tions in the Pacific Islands. 'You say that, Tommy,' one of the
wives once said, 'but you're more ambivalent than you admit.'
True, I get trapped by guilt and my conscience pursues me into
submission, into conventional behaviour. Square pegs.

Where's the art in medicine these days and how does the
artist get through medical school, or even get in? I've said it
before and I'll repeat it: some of us don't fit into the stationary
medical world, which is turning us into business people.

I've tried fitting into hierarchies with varying degrees of lack of
success. I had a great abhorrence of being part of the hospital and
competitive medical systems. I joined the Navy partly to avoid
those ridiculous scenarios, partly to pander to the wandering genes

in my blood and partly because I wanted to challenge myself in extreme situations. My first posting was on the *HMAS Hawke*, based in Fremantle on the coast of Western Australia. She was a lovely ship of four thousand tonnes, painted white like a hydro-graphic, oceanographic ship, not grey like a warship. There were no gunnery people aboard as we had no armaments, just a small crew of one hundred and fifty men.

Being isolated and remote at sea led to the sort of medical experiences I sought. We'd sailed from Fremantle one autumn day to represent Australia when the Seychelles achieved their independence from Britain. At 1900h there came a pounding at my cabin door.

'Doc, Tug Wilson's just come to sick bay,' cried Jim McGuinn, the medic. 'He's in a lot of pain. You'd better come.'

'What kind of pain?'

'Abdominal.'

Fear. Panic. Terror. My first night out on my first posting and I had visions of appendicitis and an emergency operation, with the chief executive officer doing anaesthetics and a leading sea-man assisting.

I've no memory of running from my cabin to sickbay. At the desk sat Tug Wilson, chief petty officer, bearded and balding and pale as the little white name patch on the left breast of his faded, dark blue boiler suit. Tug Wilson did not look at all well.

I hurried to the desk, grabbing a file and pen and hoping the patient didn't see my anxiety. 'Where's the pain, Tug?' The Navy had a language of its own. Various surnames automatically had a nickname. People with the surname of Wilson became Tug. We called people A-Z who had long, European-sounding names like Kowalsky.

'Right here, doc.' He poked his lower right abdomen.

'What does it feel like?'

'It hurts.'

'Is it constant or intermittent, dull or sharp?'

'It just hurts, all the time.'

'Does it hurt more when you're standing or sitting or lying down?'

'More when I get off the bunk, or try to stand up and walk around.'

'When you cough?'

'Yeah.'

'When you move around?'

'Yeah.'

'Do you feel it in any other part of your body, like your back or your leg?'

'Just me gut.'

'How's your appetite?'

'I always feel a bit off me food the first day at sea.'

'Bowel action?'

'Haven't had one today.'

'Yesterday?'

'Don't remember.'

'Alright, Tug, strip down to your shorts and socks and hop onto that table.' I nodded towards a narrow, hard, uncomfortable, wretched little operating table bolted to the floor.

Tug unfastened the one-piece boiler suit and let it slip to the floor.

'Lie on your back with your legs straight.'

He moved slowly, in obvious pain.

'Does it hurt here? Here? What about here?' I asked, checking and listening to his abdomen. He had pain and tenderness in his right iliac fossa, which meant that it might be his appendix. An emergency operation loomed closer.

'Open your mouth. Let's have a look at your tongue.'

Looked okay.

I took his temperature. He was afebrile, a point in his favour and mine. 'Roll over, on your left side and we'll do a rectal examination.'

Tug turned with the reluctance many people exhibit when about to endure this probing. 'I hope I don't fall off this thing,' he said, curling up on his side. Tug had a bit of discomfort during the rectal examination. I'm sure my anxiety and fear was apparent, which can't have been very reassuring for the patient.

After half an hour I said, 'I want you to stay in sickbay, Tug. I want to monitor you during the night.'

'Whatever you say, doc.'

Evacuating Tug Wilson by helicopter was impossible, as we were too far out to sea, beyond helicopter range of shore. I didn't want to steam back to Perth when we were supposed to be representing our country in the Seychelles, especially for what might turn out to be a case of constipation.

I did three things. First I rang a surgeon in Perth for advice. Organising a radio-telephone link was quite a business, with the radio operators pretending not to listen. Next I talked the executive officer through a hypothetical operation. 'If the situation gets worse,' I said, 'we might have to operate.' I had never done appendectomies although I'd assisted at them. Then I went back to my cabin and prayed I wouldn't become too frightened to be able to think correctly. I prayed I wouldn't make mistakes of interpretation and I prayed I wouldn't have to operate on Tug Wilson.

This was the first situation in which I really had to face terror. I've found subsequently that when you're in remote areas and faced with uncertainty, it's hard not to let your anxiety, fear or terror overwhelm you. If that happens you tend to jump to the wrong conclusions or the worst conclusions.

I had a *very* fitful sleep. Next morning I examined Tug Wilson as soon as I woke up. He was still afebrile, thank God, and we were now *way* out to sea.

I rang up the Perth surgeon again, who suggested giving him a suppository to try and relieve his bowels. He was far more experienced than I and it was a bloody relief to be able to talk to him.

I gave Tug the suppository. It had the desired effect. Sometimes all your Christmases come at once when somebody has a bowel action. Tug was okay and so was I.

The second story occurred when I breached protocol in the middle of the Indian Ocean. We've got the government breathing down our necks in various guises. Is it any wonder that some of us bolt? The Australian Navy have got instructions on how to do everything. My first rap on the knuckles came on *HMAS Hawke* between

Diego Garcia and the Seychelle Islands. I was happy that trip and felt a connection with my ancestors. In addition to the banana plantation manager, another ancestor had run a cattle-and-coconut plantation in the South Pacific whilst a third, a medico, had died on horseback one night in mysterious circumstances in the wilds of Tasmania. Our second night out from Diego Garcia, a horseshoe-shaped coral atoll at the bottom of the Maldives with an American base and some wild donkeys, I decided to have a public meeting in the main mess on the lower deck where the crew ate. I called it without obtaining the permission of the captain. This was a mistake that earned me a rap on the knuckles.

I told the crew about some of the illnesses that might be available to them and urged them to use condoms whilst ashore. 'There aren't any fancy condoms in the ship's stores,' I explained, 'just plain latex, but they are freely available.' I could be wrong, but I think the English invented condoms, originally called 'racials,' in the nineteen-twenties during the eugenics craze to stop the British working class and 'coloured people' from expanding their numbers.

The men seemed responsive and I felt gratified.

The outcome was that a number of blokes presented with the pox or the clap as soon as we left the Seychelles. They explained their problem variously, with some feeling ashamed, some seeing it as a badge of honour, some acting quite blasé and some married and worried. They all had to be treated.

One quiet little bloke said matter-of-factly, 'I've got a drippy dick, doc.'

I took a sample of Leading Seaman Beercroft's discharge, plated it out, did a gram stain and examined it under the microscope. You couldn't take a swab, bundle it off to a courier and get the lab to give you a report. You did it yourself. No mistaking that stain. The gonorrhoea bordered on being penicillin resistant, requiring massive amounts of the antibiotic. Jim McGuinn the medic and I prepared to give Leading Seaman Beercroft eight injections of penicillin, one and one-half million units of penicillin per injection, all at once, four in each buttock, on the advice of the Seychelles hospital. The acrid smell was overpowering.

'Up on the table, mate,' I said.

Beercroft dropped his football shorts, part of the crew's everyday attire, and hopped up. He looked like a skinned rabbit with his scrawny buttocks on that narrow operating table.

I positioned myself on one side and Jim McGuinn went to the other.

Beercroft didn't whimper at all, not a sound, though it must have been dreadfully painful. McGuinn and I kept jabbing those scrawny buttocks for a long time, in a rhythm quite unlike that which had got him into trouble.

'That's it, mate,' I said finally.

Beercroft got up, nodded his thanks with a wan smile and waddled out like a duck. He crept over the bulkhead and into the passageway.

I never saw him again, but it wouldn't be long before I committed another breach of protocol.

I clashed with Essence of Bureaucrat in the third story, a most malodorous encounter, whilst doing a favour for a friend who has great trouble finding locums for her remote practice. Locums are supposed to maintain the status quo, but we have ethical responsibilities to ourselves as well as our peers. Hopefully one works for a principal with the same philosophy, as nothing's worse than working for someone with lower or different standards.

'As you're going out there,' I said one night to the domiciliary sister in the nurses' station, 'can you whip out Mr Osborne's stitches and save him a sixty-mile trip?'

'Yes, doctor,' she said slowly, 'I can do it, but I've got to fill out a nine-page document for every person I visit, to comply with health department policy.'

I have some opinions on situations like this. It's not getting out of bed at two in the morning, sitting beside the road managing airways or getting locums that's killing rural medicine. It's putting up with bureaucratic intervention, especially if you're attached to a rural hospital. You've always got some bastard coming and telling your nursing staff what they can and cannot do. The only way these people can justify their jobs is by creating paperwork to justify outcomes. I hate that word, *outcomes*.

Nine pages of bureaucratic bunk just to whip out a few stitches and save a pensioner a lot of time and trouble. 'It's crazy,' I said, 'bloody bureaucrats should be–'

'Doctor!' interrupted the charge sister, holding her hand over the telephone, 'it's Mrs Neward, about Jamie.'

I took the phone. 'Dr MacDonald here.'

'Doctor, you said to ring you if Jamie got worse. It's his breathing.'

'I'll be right over.'

I grabbed my bag and bolted out the door, calling over my shoulder, 'Have the ambulance meet me there.'

The fog was in, rolling off the river and making the headlights glow. The ambulance and I pulled up in front of the Newards' old miner's cottage at the same time. I didn't know one of the ambulance officers but I'd met the driver many times.

'I think we'll need to take Jamie to town, Jack,' I said after examining the boy. Those ambulance officers are just fantastic. Jack had been the volunteer ambulance driver for the last twenty-seven years, seeing the old doctor out and my friend in. 'He's having arrhythmias.'

Twenty minutes later we were whizzing down the highway, sirens wailing and lights flashing. Jamie was stabilised but still pretty sick and I stayed in the back with him. After some time, I realised that we'd left the river and its fog far behind us. Stars packed the bowl of night, nearly touching the ground. God I love the country. I couldn't live in town. I loathe the place. I knew my principal felt the same and wished she could sail a thirty-two foot canoe-stern sloop round the south coast doing a few locums, a bit of bush-walking and a lot of talking to trees.

'One of the city-based ambulances will be meeting us for the transfer, doc,' Jack said, breaking into my reverie. He slowed down to twenty kilometres an hour. I unbuckled my seat belt and went over to Jamie to give him some comfort, as he was quite unwell and afraid, poor little bloke. I'd feel better when he was in hospital.

We got Jamie into the waiting vehicle with the help of the other ambulance officer. 'You'll be right, mate,' I assured the little boy before jumping out and slamming the door.

Suddenly I felt a cold hand on my arm. 'Just a minute, doctor,' said the ambulance officer from town.

I turned. 'Yes?'

'I am the occupational health and safety officer for the western division of the state ambulance service,' he said. Why he acted so proud of it was beyond me.

'I am very concerned about your restraint situation in the ambulance.'

'What do you mean?'

'You were in the back with the patient, and you stood up while the vehicle was in motion. Do not attempt to deny this. I saw you. This is very dangerous and sets a bad example for the community when members of our health profession–'

Here he was with a decompensated kid, giving me a lecture on occupational health and safety.

I did the only thing a sane person could possibly do. I climbed into our ambulance and called over my shoulder, 'F*** off.' My principal wasn't in the least upset when I told her what had happened, and in fact said she wished she'd had the guts to do it herself.

The family bosom

Noose Grimeley

'It's corroding me,' Noose Grimely said, using the heel of his open palm to hit his reddish-blond eyebrows, which began profusely over his nose and ended sparsely at his temples. 'Every time I see a patient, I wonder if this will be the one to sue me. Will it be the obnoxious old misanthrope with the Filipina bride and stubborn earwax? The righteous young mum with the neurotic child? Someone I least suspect, the relative of a favourite patient perhaps? Patients are obsessed with their rights. What about responsibilities? I'll tell you about responsibilities.'

WE NEED A REVOLUTION. We need to put people in charge of education who have got some standards and will help to educate us out of the culture of rights we have in this country. Everybody's got rights. Rights, rights, rights. Bloody hell! Go to Burma and see who's got any bloody rights. Or anywhere in Central Africa. Why should we have rights and not them? What about responsibilities? One of our patients knew all about that.

'I'd better show you an interesting family,' remarked my senior partner, Dr Hendrickson, just before lunchtime Friday at the end of my first week. Settling in professionally had been easy; domestic reality was a different matter altogether.

'I'll just ring Christy,' I said to Dr Hendrickson. 'She's expecting me home for our son's first birthday party.' This would be the first rumbling of an avalanche of unmet family obligations and recriminations.

A little later, Dr Hendrickson and I hit the pavement. 'What makes this family interesting?' I asked, struggling to forget the avalanche of hurt silence at the other end of the telephone.

'You'll see,' Dr Hendrickson replied with a smile.

We walked briskly down streets with Victorian houses atop hills necklaced by steep gardens. I've always loved rambling Victorian houses, with twists and turns and turrets and heavy cornices, and I loved working in such houses. As we trotted through the long shadows of another age, I felt that I had truly arrived.

The bay below us glittered like a serrated knife. Dr Hendrickson and I verbally dissected the morning's patients. That bulldog Mr Pugh, whom we called Mr Pughnacious, had again asserted humourlessly that his rights extended to use of the staff tearoom. Mrs Bon-Anibotty, whom we called the Good Antibody, had reminded us urgently of her *raison d'etre*, wheelchair access to fast-food restaurants. Personally, I think people who go to such places deserve to have slippery steps, barking Dobermans meeting them as they arrive and food poisoning as they leave.

Rights, rights, rights. 'What about responsibilities?' I said to the bay. My wife would have found this statement ironic.

'You're about to learn about that,' Dr Hendrickson answered.

How right he was. Patients can be a bloody terrifying responsibility. I should have gone into farming.

'I try to look in on this family regularly,' he said. 'It's hard for them to come to the surgery.'

We crossed behind a glass factory into a winding cul-de-sac with fifteen homes on each side. They were standard weatherboard, single storey two- and three-bedroom houses. Low-grade and no hot water. Not a garden in sight, although the odd clump of brave grass managed to survive. In front of our destination, the only two trees on the street supported each other in a twisted embrace. From the house issued the most almighty commotion. If my wife saw this, perhaps she'd stop whingeing about the expensive European trees and shrubs she needed for the garden. Tree peonies, for God's sake? Why on earth would a Himalayan native want to take root here?

Dr Hendrickson hopped the low step to the porch and banged at the door.

Sounds of barking greeted his knock.

'Ah!' I cried delightedly. 'I've always been partial to dogs.'

He looked over and raised his eyebrows.

I cocked an ear but couldn't place these dogs. One of my little conceits has always been an ability to identify a dog from its bark. A minor talent, admittedly, but it lassoed more than one date in the old days. 'Our own breed of rare dogs! What a country!'

Dr Hendrickson smiled. 'Yes.'

'Two, three,' I counted. 'Perhaps I could get one.'

'No need. You'll be caring for these soon enough.'

'Four!' In my excitement, the import of his statement eluded me.

Heavy human footfall, the muffled sounds of grunting kicks and yelps of pain escaped the opening door.

Misgivings surfaced.

'Do they bite?' I asked.

'No, but they lick a lot,' my partner said, trying not to smile.

The door opened a crack.

'Yeah? Oh, hello, doc,' grunted a medium-sized man with a pronounced small head. 'Down!' he said, gently shove-kicking something behind him.

'Mr Aidan Lombardo, this is Dr Grimely. He works with us now. I'm taking him round the neighbourhood. May we come in?'

'I guess so,' answered the perfectly nice chap, with that air of wide-eyed wonderment that made him unfit for the tribulations of life outside the home. 'Lemme get 'em to the lounge room first.'

I thrust myself forward to meet the dogs before Aidan could close the door. My senior partner restrained me with a hand to the shoulder.

'We'll do it his way, if you don't mind.'

'Of course not,' I replied, abashed. I had a lot to learn.

Soon an interior door banged and the barking became muffled.

I hung back. Dr Hendrickson led the way. 'Aren't they clean,' I said admiringly, noting the singular lack of dog detritus – smells, hair, bones, drool – as we traversed a narrow corridor. 'Quite a country, Dr Hendrickson.'

'It certainly is, Dr Grimely.'

Dr Hendrickson opened the lounge room door. I stopped, aghast. Something I had not encountered outside textbooks greeted me. Here were not four dogs of a rare breed but four humans who resembled animals. They all had strabismus, their squints being convergent rather than divergent, microcephaly and prominent, beaked noses. They shared joint contractures, a stiffened, persistent flexion of joints in their limbs that caused them to move around like animals, on their hands and knees.

These four men grunted but did not speak, made funny noises and kissed my calf. They were severely brain-damaged, obviously beyond any remedial help. Back then the only choices were to send them to the local mental hospital or look after them at home.

'No one is sure of their paternity,' Dr Hendrickson observed as the four brothers gathered round his legs. 'Rumour has it they had different squires and that their mother carried the flawed gene.'

The four brothers loped towards me like slow-moving greyhounds or whippets, with none of their grace. I suppressed the urge to bolt.

'Foetal alcohol syndrome?' I asked, gingerly patting an affectionate head whose tongue dribbled on my knee. From above their heads looked particularly tiny. None of their faces had the flat, flabby, expressionless, doll-like mask usually associated with foetal alcohol syndrome.

'No,' Dr Hendrickson answered, scratching their chins in turn. 'Probably inbreeding from incest over more than one generation, from some genetic or chromosomal defect.'

Inbreeding here is no different from other relatively isolated communities in the world. People get randy and no one's in sight but their own family members. All four men wore nappies, their pale and hairless legs exposed like great slabs of dead fish.

'It's summer,' Aidan explained, following my gaze. 'I try to air them out.'

'How old are they?' I asked.

'Between twenty-five and thirty-five,' Aidan answered. His life was clearly mapped.

Dr Hendrickson gestured to two of the brothers. They looked alike to me. John wore a black T-shirt with Grateful Dead scrawled on the back in magenta and a psychedelic image on the front. Paul wore a plain white T-shirt.

'John and Paul have dicky hearts,' he explained. 'Have a look at them while I examine Tom.' Dr Hendrickson gestured toward the brother wearing an electric yellow singlet, corrugated like cottage cheese, 'Tom having any more troubles with his water-works, Aidan?'

'No, doc.'

That left one brother, who wore a football jersey emblazoned with the word, Carlton.

'Tim's generally okay,' Dr Hendrickson added. 'How's your partner, Aidan?'

'She's gone again, doc,' he answered sadly. 'Took the little ones, her four 'n my two. Don't think she'll be back this time.' Looking at his brothers, he added, 'Can't say as I blame her.'

Aidan looked much older than his brothers, but stress could have caused that. And responsibility. Aidan knew all about responsibility. Using the staff tearoom or an expedition to the local fast-food restaurant were inconsequential to Aidan Lombardo. As I said, we need a revolution. Rights, rights, bloody rights.

The man who wore his dog

Amaranth Fillet

*'Hope you don't mind hanging round home. We'll have us some
fun tonight. We've got speakers out here and a stack of CDs.
Wayne's on call and I've got to monitor the quartet,' said
Amaranth Fillet. 'Job-sharing with your spouse has its moments.
Kids! Come and meet someone.' A blizzard of feet swirled onto
the veranda. 'Penniman – we call him Teddy – and Lucille, and
Sally, where's your sister? Ah! Miss Molly. That voice, Mol!
Won't you ever learn to tone it down? We're not shouting across
a paddock. That reminds me of something I must tell our visitor.
Off you go, kiddies.'*

I VAN SHOULD BE in an 'ome, doc,' his wife boomed one
day in her powerful voice, better suited to calling across pad-
docks than to traumatising the telephone.

'He doesn't want to go, Mrs Kent.'

'I can't take care of 'im no more.'

I could see Mrs Kent hovering over the telephone, anxious to
return to her chooks and garden.

'He's not much bother, really, is he, Mrs Kent?'

'He needs feedin'.'

'He can take himself to the loo. Keep him at home and I'll
look after him,' I said. 'I'll be available if ever you want me, if
I'm around.'

She did want me. By that time they were already well over
eighty. Mr Kent had spent most of his life shearing in the howling winds of desolate highland sheep country. I suspected he'd
rather be out there than bored silly sitting inside all day long
with nothing to do. His parents had pulled him from school
before he'd learned to read because they needed him to work.

His wife told me years ago that she was still angry at them for depriving her husband of a basic education. Mr Kent was as smart as anyone else, he just never had the opportunities. Now it was coming home to roost.

I was on call when the phone rang, one cold Saturday afternoon in early autumn, not long after we'd come to this practice. Leaves were starting to fall, a murmuring undertone in the wind's clamour.

'Can you come round and see 'im?' Mrs Kent bellowed down the phone.

'Yes of course, I'm on the way.'

As I stopped the car near the gate, Mrs Kent straightened from weeding a row of leeks and waved. I love to see a good vegetable garden when I visit patients. It tells me they're looking after themselves. It doesn't cost much, just a bit of time weeding and watering. I feel sad about the people inside if I see a run-down garden and have to fight my way through a tangle to the front door.

Until I get to know people quite well, I always make a point of going to the front door. Sometimes it's never used for any purpose other than letting in the doctor. Many of my colleagues go round the back and burst in, but you don't know what you're interrupting.

Mrs Kent wore her usual attire: an ankle-length dress covered by a full apron with a print pattern and two pockets riding the bulge of her tummy – and what a bulge it was. As always she wore black, flat-heeled shoes that rooted her firmly to the earth.

I'd been able to convince the good woman to keep her husband at home, but for how much longer?

I reached into the back seat. I didn't think I'd need to take much with me. Old Ivan didn't want what was in my bag. His needs were different. Mrs Kent left her garden only reluctantly long after dark. If there's a garden equivalent of the term house-proud, then Mrs K was it. I can picture her yet, trowel in one hand, packet of seeds in the other, wisps of straw in her hair and two great patches of dirt at her knees.

'Go on in doc, he's in the room there,' Mrs Kent called in that mighty voice, like one of those wonderful American black gospel singers, 'and I'll get you some eggs.'

That was the entire introduction to her husband's latest crisis. I went through the back door into the house. It was old but very clean, with a sink in the corner of the main living area. They'd slung a bar across the open fireplace. A huge, cast-iron pot always hung from the bar. I marvelled at the weight it held, especially Mrs Kent's stews and curries. Many's the time that rabbit juice bubbled over and sizzled the red-hot coals below because Mrs Kent was busy outside.

I looked around as my eyes became accustomed to the dimness. An old fellow sat in an older armchair. A television was switched on but he wasn't watching it. He'd buried his chin in his chest and was rugged up like nobody's business. He'd a hat on and a scarf round his neck.

I couldn't tell what was wrong. 'I'll wake him up,' I thought, grabbing hold of one hand and shaking him a bit.

Mr Kent slowly opened one eye, then just as slowly closed it again.

I decided to unwrap him from all those things. First I removed his old beanie. So far so good. Trouble soon surfaced. I reached for the furry-looking thing encircling Mr Kent's neck.

I touched it.

The scarf moved and jumped.

'Ah!' I cried, leaping back with both arms raised protectively.

Ivan laughed, showing his decayed teeth. In those days men chewed tobacco, which stained their mouths with nicotine and rotted their teeth.

The scarf ran off with nary a sound.

Ivan laughed some more.

I've never got such a shock in my life!

By this time Ivan was laughing quite hard.

It was a border collie!

Poor old Ivan. He just sat there in that cold room in the middle of the day, with the fire gone cold and his wife gone, well, outside in the garden. He laughed and laughed, his teeth the same colour as his sheepdog's.

I suppose he should have been in a home, but it would have killed him. It wasn't too bad, really, for Mrs Kent. He didn't give her much bother. He just sat in his chair, a fading farm animal past his use-by date. I'll never, ever forget that border collie draped round the old shearer's neck.

'They always sit there together like that,' Mrs Kent said from the doorway. She showed no surprise at my outburst. 'They're great mates.'

'Good way to keep warm,' I said, imagining that soft ripple of fur round my neck.

'He always rode to work on his bicycle with his dog around his neck,' his wife said. 'They always travelled like that.'

I wondered if the dog would so accompany the old shearer on his last journey as I began my physical examination.

'Since you're here, doctor'

E Manley Dew

'People need help to make it through the night, in my experience,'
said E Manley Dew, 'and that often means drink, which can slip
so easily into abuse.' She climbed onto a boulder, jagged with
footholds. 'There was Mr Nilsson, whom I found crawling by the
roadside one day. I nearly ran him down,' she said, uncorking a
bottle of red wine and pouring it into plastic goblets. 'But let me
set it up properly. It began in my childhood.'

ONE DAY, after the leaves of the English oak dominating
the paddock had bronzed, Mother took a chance on
Martha. Our last childhood cleaner saw us through the
growing-up years. She'd had a rough life. One of the reasons,
they said in those days, was her inability to bear children.
Mother said this was a Blessing or she'd pop them out like her
sisters and then would have No Chance. Mother never said for
what.

Patients were different then, less feral. Mother solved the
problem of particularly needy ones by hiring them, something
now out of the question. As an example, two of Martha's prede-
cessors stand out from the cavalcade of domestics and handy-
men who taught us the facts of life. Kathleen was a large, wheezy
lady who collapsed into cigarette breaks on closed white toilet
seats, huffing and puffing about her arthuritis. Kathleen never
quite coped with the curves and hooks life threw at her. She
smoked up the house and didn't last long.

Then there was Judy Onions, who possessed too many curves
for Mother's liking. Her love life lurched from one youthful
drama to the next. I listened to tantalising mumblings as Judy's
cloth squeaked over mirrors in tight, vicious circles. She inspected

her face in quadrants in the resulting sheen. I drifted to the mirror to search for what she found so fascinating, but whatever it was went with her. My brothers looked at Judy in a special way. She didn't last long, either.

Unlike her curvaceous predecessor, Martha never peered into the bathroom mirror. The plain rectangle tacked above the basin, unadorned by frame or flower, held no fascination for the fading woman. Accelerating the dimming process was a layabout husband who received an invalid pension that he spent down at the pub with his mates. He'd buy several crates of beer on Saturday – at a shilling a bottle – and sell them on Sunday mornings, which were dry, for five shillings a bottle. I can hear Dad telling Mother during the morning shaving ritual, leaning into the mirror with his lathered chin sticking out, 'I say to the chaps, "Why not buy a few bottles extra and put them aside so you don't have to buy them for five shillings a pop?" "They never last, doc. We drink 'til we run out."'

Our series of cleaners and their alcoholic relatives instilled in me empathy and tolerance. That brings me back to the story I was going to tell you about the patient crawling to the pub. Soon after I'd come to this practice, I was driving home for lunch one winter's day – we used to have enough time to drive home for lunch in those days. The hours are much longer now and we're more isolated. At any one time, we're all in our rooms communicating with the patients. We have to intrude into that relationship to communicate with each other.

That day, I nearly drove over one of my patients. He was making his way on hands and knees down the road, on the way to his local pub two blocks away.

'What,' I asked in my sternest voice, 'do you think you're doing?' I always liked Mr Nilsson, despite our long history of middle-of-the-night alcoholic phone calls.

'I need a drink,' he rasped, 'and *She* won't give me one.' Mr Nilsson looked like a much-loved teddy bear, battered round the edges but indispensable. Mr Nilsson had escaped from his wife. He'd come of age in the days when drinking was a serious occupation in which everybody indulged. You drank, and drank heavily.

In my practice, people drank beer. You weren't a proper person unless you drank beer. Mr Nilsson preferred brandy. And he was serious about it.

'In you go,' I said, stretching across to open the passenger door. Over the years I've seen as many kinds of alcoholics as there are people. Mr Nilsson didn't leave it 'til the weekend and beat his wife. Drink never turned him nasty. Nor did he hoard beer on a Saturday to make a few bob on a Sunday. Mr Nilsson just drank and drank and drank. He lost his job as the managing director of a big firm in the city and then built himself up again from scratch in the same firm. They started him off as a counter hand. He worked his way up to sales manager. Eventually he retired from work, resumed his drinking and moved to a less than desirable neighbourhood.

I delivered Mr Nilsson to his wife, a quiet woman whom I admired – she'd stayed with her husband through better and now worse.

As I headed for the car, a woman ran up from the house next door, typical of the dwellings in this area. These were people who had sunk to the bottom of the pile, beaten down by events. For all sorts of reasons they had lost community support. This may have been from their bad behaviour. They were housed – reluctantly – by the state government. They never paid rent because they had no income. There was no mother-supporting pension. If Dad was in jail, as many of the husbands of these people were, you had no income.

'Good afternoon, doctor. Fine day, but a bit cold,' the woman said.

'It certainly is, Mrs Birley,' I replied, waiting.

'Since you're here, doctor,' she said, with a certain firm set to her mouth. This woman remained alone after the smoke had cleared on the alcoholic battlefield that claimed her husband. She reminded me of the childhood parade of the walking wounded (Walking Wounded, Mother would say) through our home.

At those awful words, I bid goodbye to what was left of my lunch break.

'It's Meg.'

'Yes?'

'She's not too well. Could you spare just a moment?' The tiny Mrs Birley looked like a toy nanny, with hair coiled tightly round her head and hands ready to fuss, pet or whack. Her hands always fascinated me, with their air of better times.

'Certainly,' I replied, following her inside. 'How are your sons?' I'd forgotten their names but remembered hearing bad news.

'Still in prison for murder,' she said softly.

I wondered, as I had for years, how so delicate a woman could have produced those two brutes. They were unruly and obnoxious, even as children.

'They're both in for twenty-five more years interstate,' she continued. 'They aren't bad boys, just headstrong. They can't hold their liquor.'

Kevin and Kurt smoked whatever was going and drank Southern Comfort, Bacardi, and cask wine in large quantities. One of them had tried unsuccessfully to blackmail me emotionally into writing prescriptions for drugs used by and sold to abusers. They reminded me of Martha's husband's drinking mates.

Mrs Birley had taken another step down the social ladder by coming to this weatherboard, single storey three-bedroom house in which she and her daughter rented a bedroom. This was The Avenue, a cul-de-sac behind an old nurses' home with a dozen low-grade houses without hot water systems, only the minimum amenities needed for survival. Families in dire straits lived here, soon to be put out on the streets to find their own accommodation.

'Sorry for bothering you, doctor. I didn't want to bring Meg out in this weather.'

Listening to the child's cough, I could understand why.

'How old are you, Meg?'

'Twelve, doctor.'

Meg was a fine-looking girl, with blond hair and freckles sprayed across her nose and cheeks.

'What a lovely young lady,' I said as I percussed Meg's chest. Her mannerisms and speech bespoke high intelligence. 'Not at all like her brothers.'

'Ah well, doctor,' Mrs Birley said, smiling for the first time I could remember, 'I used to be a shorthand typist.'

In the social strata of Mrs Birley's childhood years, achieving the status of shorthand typist required considerable diligence. She probably had a reasonable social background to enable her to be educated and rise beyond the typing pool.

'What happened?'

'I got pregnant,' she replied, 'and then it was downhill all the way.'

In those days you didn't marry the wrong guy and have two kids, get a pension, toss him out, get a flat from the government and rear your children in a peaceful life. You reared twelve children with a brutal husband and you could not get away. If you were lucky like Mrs Birley, the booze-soaked bounder deserted the family, never to be heard from again.

Meg coughed.

The place smelled of damp. I looked up and saw the reason.

'I asked the council to fix the leaks in our roof,' Mrs Birley said, fighting back tears. 'They said they were gong to close the house.'

'By not upgrading or repairing, they can get rid of tenants,' I said.

People round here tended to be basic by anybody's standards, but they varied enormously in their abilities, especially the women. Some were extremely skilled people who had fallen on bad times, like Mrs Birley.

'I asked them to relocate us. Meg and I have nowhere else to go. Maybe we should move interstate so I can see my boys on visiting days.'

'Returning Meg to the orbit of those two brothers might prove disastrous,' I said.

She nodded, eyes on the ground.

I recalled the childhood cleaners I'd loved and to whom I felt closer than to the women of our family. They waded through a world that wasn't such a good fit. The female relatives – the good wives, physiotherapists, nurses and practice managers – lacked a dimension of bewilderment with which I identified. Mother would have hired Mrs Birley in some capacity. She'd never have left that woman and child adrift. I made my living as a healer, but did I have her basic compassion?

A mother screamed at a toddler on the porch. All was quiet in the Nilsson household.

'I can't read your mind, dammit'

Zoltan Nagy

'Ah, New Orleans! I love this place. Tourists, pavement artists and more tourists by day. Dixieland, Cajun and church music, all heard from this one spot by night, like now. I can almost smell the hay on that Midwesterner with the protruding abdomen, the salt spray from that sour New Englander's sailboat and the paints on the palette of that nomad doing pastel sunsets on the sidewalk ... What? Do not be rude to your elders, pet,' said Zoltan Nagy, wriggling his toes luxuriously in his buttery loafers. 'It may smell of dead cow to you, but your generation has no taste in footwear, let alone gloves – no taste at all. For you it is mad cow or old cow – ah! That reminds me of a patient.'

Mrs ANGELICA GEE was unremarkable in every way, except one. She carried a grudge, carried it like a lead-and-glass cross, through good times and bad.

'Can't you leave the telly on, doctor?' Mrs Gee asked from the depths of her sickbed with no good grace. Patients resent having the blasted thing turned off and this good woman was no exception.

Her little black dog, Nikki, marked the occasion by nipping at my ankle. It was the same breed as the Babbadges' dogs – about which Thucydides Hare expounded many a time – but unlike them was not allowed to leave exuberant reminders scattered about. I kicked it away surreptitiously.

'This is a medical consultation. I do not have the television on in my office so why should I allow it to be on here?'

'I don't know why Tiff had to get you out,' she grumbled, eyes on the TV.

'What is the problem, Mrs Gee?' I suspected a psychological cause for her steady deterioration.

Mrs Gee was spitting chips. 'Tiffany's so terrible,' she said, adding a sizzle to her daughter's name.

'What do you mean?' I asked.

Mrs Gee's daughter seemed quite a reasonable lady of thirty or so, not at all florid and emotional like her mother and grandmother but pale and silent like her long-dead father.

The widow drew herself up regally. Her chins followed reluctantly. 'She *will* keep using my washing machine,' she said. Threaded through her arms and shoulders was a hand-knitted shawl in a shade of pink best abandoned by any female over the age of five.

'Why is that?'

'They sold everything to go overseas. When they came back she was pregnant and they got this flat and had my grandson,' Mrs Gee explained with another longing glance at the television.

I've never got used to coming second to a box.

'I said she could come to my house and use my washing machine, 'cause they hadn't got one.'

'Yes?'

'And she's still using it.'

'So?'

'But the child's two now.' She nodded toward a photo on the dresser near the door. It held the obligatory photos, only one of everything: grandson, her own wedding and two little girls. Absent were Mr Gee and her daughters as adults.

'Did you put a time limit on using the washing machine?'

Mrs Gee paused. 'No.'

'Have you told Tiffany it's about time she bought her own washing machine?'

'No.'

'Then how is she to know that she should not be using yours?'

'Well, she ought to know.'

'She cannot read your mind,' I said.

'Oh.' Silence. 'I suppose not,' she said.

'If you do not want her to use your washing machine, you have got to tell her.'

'Oh.' This woman had never thought things through.

Little knitted dolls populated the room. A while back there was a craze for knitting penguin jumpers, to keep the little darlings warm. Mrs Gee preferred dolls. At least they looked like dolls. They may have been voodoo ritual objects. Mrs Gee was easily offended.

'Most daughters will happily use their mothers' washing machines if they are silly enough to let them,' I said, idly picking up a doll from the dresser, 'just as some friends will abuse our trust.' Was it my imagination or did Mrs Gee shoot the floppy image in my hand a fleeting look of furtive triumph?

'She's not wearing out her own money,' Mrs Gee said righteously. She looked exactly like her mother, a massive and empurpled woman who defied us medicos and lived far longer than we predicted. La mère had what she called 'high blood.' It didn't get her in the end. That honour went to complications from a broken hip.

'And then there is your privacy,' I said.

'That's exactly right, isn't it Nikki?' The dog yipped its agreement. 'She invades me with dirty clothes. Haven't I put in enough years at it? And the smell! That's the worst thing.'

Mrs Gee would not have thrived in the Babbadge household, with its putrefying male body parts and pellets of doggie mementos. Nikki would not have survived in this household unless she ate and defecated at her mistress's whim. Did people make canine effigies? This was not the home of free-roaming dogs, oh no, not here, and certainly not Mrs Gee's bedroom.

Disintegration threatened the entire mother–daughter relationship because Mrs Gee's daughter still used the washing machine when her mother had told her to do so. No wonder the poor girl had rung me.

In an effort to make the point, I took us back in time. 'Do you remember when you came in with Tiffany and her sister about ten years ago?' I recalled a woman – with a stern twist to her mouth, an aggrieved sensitivity in her eye and a frightening ledge of bosom – who shepherded her two girls into the consulting room like a mother duck.

Like Mrs Babbadge in her early incarnation as the pregnant Rosie, Mrs Gee had disowned a daughter. She now had the good grace to look sheepish. During that long-ago consultation, Mrs Gee refused to speak to Tiffany. She spoke to the other daughter, who transmitted the message.

Curiosity had got the better of me. 'Why don't you speak to Tiffany?'

'I haven't spoken to her for years,' came the brisk reply.

'Is that true?' I had asked the appropriate daughter.

'Yes,' she replied.

'Why, what is the problem?'

Mrs Gee and Tiffany looked at one another. Then they looked at the other daughter and asked, 'What was it about?' The three of them sat there for the next ten minutes trying to work it out, but they could not remember. By the time they left, mother and daughter were speaking.

That Sunday morning, my examination showed nothing physically wrong. 'You need to look after yourself, Mrs Gee,' I said. 'You are a sensitive woman. How would you feel if something happened to Tiffany?' I was thinking of a lovely patient, Jacqueline, whom I had lost just before her twenty-first birthday through lack of communication although, with the aid of the retrospectroscope, nothing could have saved her.

'I'm thirsty,' said Mrs Gee from her bed. As I handed her a glass of water in a knitted cover, she plucked a clean straw from a cylinder on the bedstand. 'I always use 'em, for hot and cold both,' she explained between sips.

I would never have gleaned this useful fact had I not visited the widow at home. 'You would never forgive yourself, would you, if something happened to Tiffany and you weren't speaking?'

'Noooo, I suppose not, but doctor, my other daughter wants to move back home for a while.'

'Absolutely not,' I said, responsive to what I thought my patient needed.

'She's just left her husband.'

'Let her go to friends. You tell her your doctor insists that your health is too precarious at the moment.'

'Oh doctor, it's not been easy.'

'I know, my dear,' I said. 'You need to rest and get your strength back.'

'I do so hate to refuse my girls anything.'

'You are a wonderful mother. No one could say otherwise.'

She darted a look of malignant satisfaction at one of the dolls. 'Yes doctor, it's a burden on my nerves, my ability to be right so often, a real cross to bear, if only you knew.' She sighed and sank back into the pink vastness of quilt and shawl.

'If you could just let others know ...' I said.

'Perhaps you're right, doctor. If my nerves were calmer, it would help, wouldn't it?' she asked, brightening. 'Do you have a nerve pill I can take?'

A guiding hand

Hugh Page-Russell

'In here,' Hugh Page-Russell bellowed, indicating a cubicle in the sex shop. 'Did a year in Nigeria when the wife left me.' He closed the door behind us and spoke into the sulphurous darkness. It was a lonely room, full of people's solitary smells. 'We're back together. Outlasted her and that toyboy. And me and Gloria. Still paying for that. Both of us. In different ways. Glad I've got the memory. Better than the reality.' He shone a torch on a notebook he unwrapped. 'I'll read this to you,' he said, opening the manuscript to page one. 'Different style.'

I'M AT OUR SHACK in the bush thinking about Nigeria and the other places I've worked, like Pakistan. Need to clear my head so I go out the back door, hopping down two wooden steps narrow as a blackbird's coffin. Flee the magic circle, past the lighted kitchen window of our holiday home, onto a dusty track. **Wattles** coat the treetops with a plum-coloured patchwork. Seedpods carpet the path, purple with black eyes. Small leaves rasp. Large ones grind. I fork from the track's compacted earth to the forest's spongy floor, following a croaking frog. The quality of light changes. Exuberant green becomes misty and quiet. Rusty splotches stain the trunk of one old gum. The tree canopy towers far above. An army of sassafras trees stands frozen in primeval time. Fuzzy lichens clump on the trunks. Lacy ones sway in the breeze. Not all trees stand upright. Some lean, elbowed and deformed by the stout branches of stronger siblings. A **currawong's** caw tunnels back thousands of years. A fallen tree forms an accidental bridge over the river.

Across I go, one foot in front of the other, arms outstretched for balance. The mossy trunk fell long before humans brewed up the current batch of troubles to poison themselves and the earth. Bluish gums, blackish myrtles and dense dark blackwoods abound. Ancient manferns dance like modest mushrooms, their lacy skirts of fronds draping thick shafts. A clump of trees bends over a waterfall, a wall of liquid glass plummeting toward river rocks below. An unseen stream emits a lower rumble.

Three more steps and I'm across. The quality of sound changes, softer around the edges, coated in wombat fur. No more echidna spikes. River roar dulls to an undulating lull. A cockatoo screeches overhead. No more croaking frog, but Smoking Frog, the Mayan general who founded a dynasty.[9] Archaeologists found piles of marine toad remains near Mayan temples. Priests used their venom to alter the consciousness of humans about to be sacrificed. I've been reading about frogs lately. Frog goddesses hopped through ancient Egypt and Mexico and still hold up the world for some people in India. Chinese believed frogs swallowed part of the moon during lunar eclipses.

'Leave all this? I couldn't. Return to Pakistan or Nigeria? Not so sure anymore,' said Dr Page-Russell when I looked at him questioningly. 'Don't be fooled. Things are not what they seem.'

A bit more tramping brings me to my spot, a shaded park with straight-boled trees and a long green view, occasionally interrupted by the umbrella of a man fern. Soil and tree-root systems have fused into red fibrous peat. I rest on a tangle of roots at the base of a beloved myrtle and gaze into the river. A giant rock in the river shimmers with moss and looks like a map of Nigeria.

Nigeria's been on my mind, with its return to democracy and sentencing to death by stoning of two women who gave birth outside marriage. My memories of that country are intimately connected with love, duty and the weather. There were four seasons: cold, followed by hot, followed by rainy in April or May, followed by the harvest season towards the end of the rains. Illness was tethered to economics. The hospital was always quieter in the rainy season, because people were farming their corn and guinea corn crops and didn't have time to get their hernia operations. The surgical schedule was quieter and outpatient numbers down. This coincided with the North American summer and the long school break, so surgeons like Chang Crowther spent time with their children.

'Fancy myself a writer. Like it?' He winced. 'See from your face. Better tell you about it instead.' He snapped the notebook shut.

Not good enough. That's the way I felt. Not for a healer. Had to leave Nigeria in the end, and it was nothing to do with the weather.

Start with the weather. Everything does there. Parched and brown in the dry season. *Harmattan's* a cold wind that blows down from the Sahara. It brings dust, a fine dust that covers everything from November to March. Light some days. Saw the haze. Others it was heavy and foggy and you couldn't see trees outside the door. Had to dust the house more than once a day, but it still got in. No matter how hard I tried. In Nigeria, the contents of a bookcase cleaned annually would be caked with dust. Had to blow it away or wash hands after reading. Same in the savannah. The trees – many eucalypts – and the ground. Everything was dingy and brown. Static electricity every time I touched a door handle. I earthed myself before working on a computer. Static charges were a possible problem in theatre, if you were using ether or oxygen. We had a few fires, probably not due to static electricity. I remember a blanket. The room lit up when I shook it. Sparks everywhere. Can't forget the sounds of the city. Carried at night. Heard noise from all over. Traffic. Parties. Music. Mostly music. And televisions. Don't notice it in the rainy season.

Rains coming transformed everything. The first one washed away all the dust. Sky was clear and blue. If not rainy or with a bit of cloud. You could see long distances. Grass sprang up. Green by June or July but raining constantly. Rains eased off late September. Weather warm and sunny. Countryside still green. Beautiful time to go travelling, as Chang Crowther knew.

Didn't see much seasonal variation in illness patterns, with a few major exceptions such as meningococcal meningitis. It sweeps through sub-Saharan Africa every March or April and strikes tens of thousands of people. Never makes the news. Wasn't a major problem in the early 1980s, but widespread later in the decade. Malaria in the rainy season. Burns in the cold season. People used open fires and kerosene heaters. Kids knocked 'em over and drank kerosene or got burnt.

Lived in a city on a volcano where people practiced spiritism. Spirit stories attached to big volcanic structures. More in rural areas. Always present. I only encountered traditional healers indirectly. Some had a herbal basis to their practice. Effective but not subject to analysis or research. Others were more religious and intricately involved with spirit worship. Traditional healers could be quite wealthy. Patients paid 'em well. I didn't personally charge. The hospital charged patients and paid me a salary. Flat rate and charity fund.

Met Gloria there. She was on her way to an outstation. She dreaded it. Feel guilty about what happened. Think of her every time I see a certain fast-food restaurant. We promised each other a good time in a forbidden McPalace one day. I couldn't stop what happened to that extremely talented theatre sister. She loved operating and should have been a surgeon. Told off a macho surgeon in London. Walked off the job. But she was fated to encounter a certain type.

Dr Chang Crowther was the most renowned expatriate in West Africa. Made his reputation during an encounter with an elephant. Cemented it during The Battle of the Hippo, as locals called it. Very skilful with sharp noisy *implements de guerre*. People drove from all over the country to consult him. Had operated under conditions through which only a Higher Hand could have guided. Then he received the type of injury he was especially gifted at repairing. Doubly ironic that he needed assistance from a gifted nurse with a grudge against his type of surgeon.

Gloria always prefaced the tale with Chang in Lagos. She heard stories. So did I. Chang escaped as soon as he could from that polluted hellhole created by oil money. Like the rest of us. Not for him urban life. Never know it by looking at him. Prototype for exhibition-opening man. Black-tie man. Bookshop-browsing man.

No, he liked his fish alive and squirming on his hook, not impaled on a toothpick at embassy parties. Chang had a countryman's self-containment. Didn't confide in anybody – especially women. Not for him remorse. That military surgeon who told his favourite nurse he feared his profession blunted his sensibilities. Rendered him indifferent to the sight of pain. Don't mean to imply insensitivity. Not Chang. No one could be as sympathetic to patients. Nor as critical of family and staff. Charming smile after a session of emotional brutality. Admission sufficient to right any wrong. He bore the cross his God had given him, but he always preferred the company of men in situations that required silence or minimal talk.

One dry season, after a bureaucratic chore in Lagos, Chang decided to reward himself. It was January. School holidays. He kissed his wife and two young daughters and set off with his mates and two teenaged sons. He had a favourite spot way up the bush where he fished for *giwan ruah*. *Giwa* is Hausa for elephant. *Ruah* means water. Stayed the usual week. They did the things men do. When the time came to leave, the elder Crowther boy threw a tantrum near the fishing hole. Surprised everybody, including himself. Was he attuned to his father in the way of firstborn sons? Did he sense upcoming danger? The Crowther fishing party stopped at a village to visit friends. There was a remote clinic servicing a few hundred people. That's where Gloria worked. Heart of the fifteenth-century pepper trade with the Portuguese. The *harmattan* blew hard that day, straight off the desert. The land a swirl of red dust. Villagers laying a water pipe – a potentially lethal activity in a developing country. Chang, his mates and sons hopped out of their Jeep as a crane lifted some large pipes. Chang offered to help. The chain broke.

'Watch out!' screamed the elder son.

Chang looked up. Glanced away quickly. Started to run. A pipe fell near him. Bounced up. Hit him in the face. Large nasty laceration to his lip. Fractured maxilla.

Never forget Gloria's words. No suture material in the clinic. Few instruments. Not good ones. Scissors blunt. The one needle rusty. Copious supply of local anaesthetic determined the nurse and the surgeon to have a go. Improvised suture material – the braid local women used on their hair. Soaked it. Got on with the job. Gloria repaired the damage, layer by layer. Chang held a mirror and gave her detailed instructions. 'That's the muscle layer. Stitch that one now.' Often tried to imagine Gloria's feelings. 'Now go to the subcutaneous. Now the skin. No, that's not right, put one there and one there.' Result was an excellent repair job.

Chang didn't help Gloria when the bullets flew. After all that. He was off somewhere, saving murderers' lives. I stopped working for a while. Couldn't overcome the bitterness. Didn't know what I'd do if I encountered Gloria's killers. That's not good enough for a healer.

The electric kettle graveyard

E Manley Dew

'Mind your step. Easy to twist an ankle,' said E Manley Dew.
We wandered through a myrtle grove. Tree roots crisscrossed the
path like stiffened spaghetti. Tiny dark leaves dappled the
sunlight. A row of dogwoods shot from a fallen tree. Serrated
sassafras leaves and tubes of bark like chocolate curls crunched
underfoot. E Manley leaned over to caress a fungus with a
lemony stem and gold umbrella, which shot from the lichen on a
nearby stone. She peered into my panting face, put down her pack
and said, 'I could use a break myself.' She cocked an ear and
smiled. 'I always think of Dimity Dell when I hear frogs.'

D ONALD DELL once did something he later regretted.
And Donald loved his wife more than most.

The phone rang at two o'clock one morning, middle
of winter, freezing cold.

'This is the constable, doctor. A man here says he's your
patient. He's holding us at bay with a gun.'

'Who is it?' I asked sleepily.

'Mr Donald Dell.'

'Yes, he and his wife are my patients,' I said, instantly alert.
'They're normally nice, quiet people. What's happened?'

'They had an argument and he had pushed her out of the house
in her nightgown and bare feet and told her if she came back, he'd
shoot her. She went to the neighbours and they called us.'

'What do you want from me?'

'Can you come and cool him down?'

'What have you done so far?'

'We wanted him to put his gun down and come out but he told
us that if we stepped inside the front gate we were dead men.'

I went out, blasting the heater in the car. Soon my fingers thawed enough for me to focus. The Dells were a childless couple in their late thirties. I had a lot of time for them. Don Dell was a typical battler. He didn't have much. They lived in the weatherboard house in which Dimity had grown up, near a river full of croaking frogs. This obviously affected her because she collected glass frogs. I'd done a home visit there one summer's evening and watched the last rays of the sun bounce off those frogs – sitting neatly in a long row – and prism into little rainbows round the room.

Both Don and Dimity had strong religious beliefs that I hoped I could draw upon now, if things hadn't gone too far. They well might have, I thought, looking at the policemen gathered in front of the neat little house. Dimity Dell leaned against one of the police cars parked at odd angles to the road.

'Has he been drinking?' I asked.

'He had a few beers earlier, doctor, but he certainly isn't drunk,' she replied. 'We were having quite a rational argument.'

I set off to the front gate.

'It's the doctor, Mr Dell,' I shouted towards the house. 'Can I come in and have a chat with you?'

'If you come on your own.'

'Now tell me what's the matter,' I said once we'd settled into the kitchen.

'Dimity keeps buying those damn electric kettles,' Don said, pointing at a bright mound of stainless steel on the benchtop. 'Then she burns out the element and goes and buys another one. I've got more bloody burned-out electric kettles in my shed – and that's just the beginning. I've never met a more extravagant woman–'

I heard his story out. I thought about the faces of consumerism. Donald Dell felt that domestic consumerism was drowning him. I felt the same about the medical variety. Medicine's got out of control. Enormous amounts of money, power and glory are available to doctors looking at the minutiae that won't make a big difference to people in the end anyway. Patients are now consumers, which we pander to by calling them clients. If patients don't get what they want from me, they'll go to down the street, or across town, or to the next town – we call it doctor shopping.

And then there's domestic consumerism, which can push even the most loving husband or wife over the edge of the marriage lifeboat.

'I just got sick of it, doc,' Mr Dell said.

'Pushing your wife out of the house at gunpoint is not a wise thing to do, Mr Dell.'

He looked sheepish.

'We need to resolve this,' I said. 'I have to have both of you in here. I need to hear her story, don't I?'

'I s'pose so.'

'Why don't we get her in, you make a cup of tea and we'll see if we can sort it out.'

'I'll use my old ceramic kettle. I don't care if it isn't good enough for Her Majesty.'

Out I went to fetch Dimity.

I told the police, 'I'll take it from here.'

'Alright, doctor,' said one of the policeman in quite a relieved tone of voice.

'Come with me, Mrs Dell. We're going to sort things out. Your husband is making us a cup of tea.'

'With the new kettle?' she asked apprehensively.

'Just follow my lead.'

'Whatever you say, doctor. I just want to get back into my warm bed.'

Poor Mrs Dell had been standing for half an hour in a filmy nightgown and matching slippers. As I held the door open for her to pass into her home I thought, not for the first time, about the loyalty of wives. This woman's husband had pushed her into the winter night at gunpoint and all she wanted was to snuggle up next to him in bed. She'd choose him all over again, I knew that. For better or worse. Dimity was loyal, like patients used to be.

Of course people have the right to choose a doctor, but they haven't the right to choose, re-choose and choose again. Consumerism has affected medicine more than litigation. Consider the classic medical response: 'We're all well trained, we're all the same.' Realistically there are some appalling doctors, but consumers aren't very good at picking them. They may think they are. The good doctor says, 'Wait and see.' Wait overnight or two weeks. More often than not that's the better medicine, but patients like what's flashy.

I sympathise with them. There's too much information available. Last week a pensioner wanted a CT scan for a headache. There's a less than one percent pickup. You can almost know that if someone's got a sudden-onset headache, it's worse in the morning and they're vomiting and they stagger into your surgery walking sideways, there's a fair chance the CT scan's going to show a brain tumour. Intermittent headaches for nine years in a patient who looks uptight, whose marriage isn't very good and whose kids are awful, well, a CT scan isn't going to show anything. And what about fashionable diseases? Consumers, fashion, it's all part of the same sick syndrome. For a while patients feared sexually transmitted diseases, then AIDS, now Alzheimer's and the ever-dreaded breast cancer.

'You married a shearing contractor, not a bloody prince,' Mr Dell said, glaring at his wife as soon as we entered the kitchen.

Dimity and I sat at the table while Don put the kettle on. 'Earl Grey for the wife,' he said. 'What about you, doc?'

'That'll be fine.'

He tossed three tea bags into ceramic mugs and set them on the table, along with a creamer and sugar bowl. Dimity jumped up to get spoons.

'Before we start I want you both to sit down, you here, Don and you here, Dimity,' I said.

They complied.

'We haven't been able to have children so far,' Mrs Dell said to me. She rose to rearrange the position of a kitchen frog beneath the window. 'Surely we can afford to replace electric kettles when they break. They're not made to last forever.'

'Two years is not forever!' Mr Dell cried. 'Why can't you just be happy with my old one? It worked fine for fifteen years before I knew you. It only needs a new element.'

I quickly mentioned their religious beliefs. 'Don't you have certain moral obligations, Don?'

'Yes.'

'Are you maintaining them with this sort of behaviour?'

'No, doctor, I suppose not.'

'Don, it's not appropriate to act as you have done.'

He looked away, his face red.

'A good marriage counsellor could help you and Dimity set realistic financial goals.'

'I wish credit cards had never been invented,' he cried.

'I can't win, Don,' Dimity snapped, closing up like a sun blossom at dusk. 'Your perception of me will never change, no matter what I do.'

'By producing a gun you bring in the police, Don,' I said, 'and once that happens there's no hope of any sort of rational discussion.'

I thought the police acted quite compassionately by not returning the next day to charge Mr Dell with threatening behaviour with a weapon. They were quite happy for me to cross the line and not so keen to do it themselves.

I keep up with Don through Dimity, who comes in regularly. She gave me a box of chocolate frogs that Christmas. It was her way of thanking me for that episode, which has not been repeated. Yet.

'Make my wife pregnant, doctor'

Yam Peale

Yam Peale looked toward the church and smiled, not a generous open-mouthed grin but a small closed circle. 'A slight leap of the imagination makes that spire look like a pen I got recently from a drug rep. Sometimes it helps to step outside of things, get a different perspective,' said the old missionary.

SHE'S NOT GETTING PREGNANT, doctor,' Mr Rai said. 'What are you going to do about it?'

Infertility in Africa and India is a huge stigma, far more socially crippling than in the West. People in developing countries have as much right to the benefits of modern technology as we do, including the latest fertility drugs. Drug testing by Western pharmaceutical companies on the world's poor is nothing new, nor are the ethical dilemmas it poses. I don't find the big pharmaceutical companies' testing of anti-malarials on Hausa-speakers in Nigeria particularly outrageous. What I'm not so sure about is fertility boosters, in either the West or developing countries. It's a question of access to resources and increasing inequality. The resource–environment–population triangle dates back to Malthus and even earlier, to the Greeks and ancient Chinese.

All that concerned the Rais was getting pregnant. I saw women in East Africa with non-specific symptoms, like feeling the heat, which could indicate depression and the diagnosis of WTBP – wants to be pregnant. The symptoms of depression are so often culturally determined.

During my years as a mission doctor, I developed a great liking for the Sikh people. British and German colonialists brought them from India in the 1800s to build railways and help run various enterprises. A lot of them had problems with fertility, as in any community. Mr and Mrs Rai came to see me at the outpatient clinic one morning, shortly after I moved my family into the city after ten years in a village mission hospital. We were part of the demographic shift from land to grand, a shift on which Mr Rai and his brothers capitalised: they ran a bus service between the outer centres and the city.

'She's not getting pregnant, doctor,' Mr Rai said. 'What are you going to do about it?'

It did not escape my notice that Mr Rai said *you*.

'There's one thing we can try,' I replied. The anxious couple leaned forward intently. The sun shimmered through Mrs Rai's sari. 'We can do a sperm count,' I said to Mr Rai.

The Rais looked at each other, then at me. Mr Rai nodded slowly, with dignity, reaching a forefinger under the back of his turban to scratch his neck.

I rummaged around under the desk. 'Take this specimen bottle and come with me,' I said.

A week later they were back. Unfortunately, the sperm test showed him to be one hundred percent fertile, as far as we could judge. I say *unfortunately* because it meant blaming his wife for the infertility.

What am I going to do now? I thought.

It did not escape my attention that I thought *I*.

At the time, one of the pharmaceutical companies marketed a preparation to stimulate ovulation and treat certain kinds of primary infertility in women. It was quite expensive and its efficacy disputed. With all this drug testing, how did one tell the good from the bad? Separating the sheep from the goats, that's the challenge.

As they faced me across the desk, the Rais provided a lovely diversion from the morning's cases of major pathology. It looked to be the usual busy morning, with one hundred and fifty to two hundred patients. The nurses and medical assistants screened them, since there was only one doctor. Patients travelled long distances, some from many hundreds of miles away. I found the young wife's sari particularly graceful, with its green-and-purple swirls and folds.

'This is a long shot,' I said, 'but if you–'

'We'll try anything, doctor,' Mr Rai interrupted.

'You realise that it's quite expensive.'

'We don't mind.'

'It may not work.'

'We have to try it.'

'It's time-consuming, a course of thirty injections over a number of months, and you cannot miss even one.'

'We'll be here, doctor.'

'It's five pounds sterling an injection.'

'Not a problem.'

'We have to give the injections at certain times of the month. You have no choice about that.'

'Fine.'

'It's very dubious. It has not ever gained favour.' I wasn't terribly keen to do it. I didn't want to waste their money or raise their hopes. Resources were not inexhaustible, either personal or common. Garrett Hardin's *Tragedy of the Commons*[10] discusses ideas I'd begun developing by that time. 'Commons' refers to resources useful to the community, like irrigation water, open-access land and sources of firewood, pasturage and fishing. Some communities have managed commons successfully in India, Africa and Latin America, but in those cases access has not been regulated. Traditions, taboos and penalties have also prevented the commons from becoming exhausted. The concept of the commons is not new. Hammu-rābi[11] in Mesopotamia, instituted legal regulations to protect the commons. Hardin argued that too many people would ruin the global commons. Some racists and environmental radicals may covertly support death, poverty and even occasional genocide because they believe this will relieve the pressure on available resources. This view is misguided.

Mrs Rai started on a course of injections the next week. To my surprise and their delight, she got pregnant in about nine months. She had two or three injections a month. That these injections worked for the Rais wasn't an unqualified triumph. The happy couple noised it abroad and I had people coming from all round East Africa. I had only one other success among many hopeful couples.

An old bushie's confession

Amaranth Fillet

'What do I want from life? I want what Little Richard wants, to be peaceable and teach love, to be remembered as one who loved people of all creeds and colours,' said Amaranth Fillet, looking past the crescent moon into a private nightscape. We were back on the road. 'Towards the end, patients sometimes question their lives. And not only at the end. We all do. I comfort them with another something Little Richard once said: the grass may look greener on the other side, but believe me, it's just as hard to cut. Sometimes patients need to get things off their chests, like Old Simon.'

TELL ME STRAIGHT, doc, this is it, isn't it?'
'Could be, Simon, could be. You never know. Miracles happen.' I badly wanted a miracle. 'Easy!' I called to the driver as we rode the thudding airstream of an overloaded log truck.

It's always been my policy to be honest with patients. Some things we tell patients and some things we don't. I think most doctors nowadays will inform a patient of cancer of the lung and say that unfortunately the tests show it's spreading. What you don't mention is, Look I'm sorry, but you are really in the final phase of this illness. You might die in the next two days.

It's not always what we tell patients. They disclose things as well. I remember an old shearer who kept pigeons, built an elaborate coop in his backyard and even had T-shirts made for his club, on which he misspelled the word *pigeon* by adding a 'd.' This man thought he was going to die from bronchitis and confessed he'd once killed an eagle, an endangered species. I assured him there were worse things he could have done.

Patients sometimes divulge things they'd never tell anyone else, not even their families – especially their families. Take Old

Simon, who'd been the best farm hand in the district. He was one of our favourite patients and a good mate of my husband. Simon and Wayne went fishing and hunting together every year. One year my husband said he thought the bushie was just too old.

Now we were in an ambulance buzzing along to the hospital. Simon lived a long way out for an old man with a bad heart. He should have been in the nursing home, but we didn't insist. We had too much respect for his autonomy. I've never liked that part of the job, restricting autonomy in the collective interest, as when we take away the licence of an elderly driver. Old Simon still lived in the house in which he'd been born. His wife had come and gone after fifty-two good years together. Simon lived on his own, except that all his departed loved ones were a big part of his life. He talked to them every day. Every corner of his home held a different conversation. We couldn't deprive him of that.

Unlike Old Simon, most people don't want to talk about imminent death, even when it's obvious. One old **Digger**, a smoker of about seventy, presented with hoarseness. I suspected throat cancer. He went off to be assessed. Late one afternoon he rang to say he was scheduled for surgery the next morning to remove his voice-box and wanted to say goodbye and thank you. He came back with a tracheotomy. By then it was too late. He was a skinny little guy with a head that looked like a skull. He also had a skin ailment, for which he had to put cream on his face that made him look like Sammy the Seal. It may have made his skin slippery but didn't diminish his status as patriarch of a large family, who all gathered round when he died. They waited twenty minutes so their mother could say farewell to her husband alone, before calling me to confirm the death.

I was thinking about the old Digger as Old Simon and I rode on what I feared would be his last journey. Simon would take a way of life with him when he went, something irretrievable. He preferred the rhythms of nature to the whirr of computers and instant communication.

'I arranged things with the bank manager, but couldn't get through to me bloody lawyer,' he said.

'I can't reach mine, either, mate,' I replied.

Old Simon was fantastically brave. They're nearly all brave at the end. I couldn't tell Simon he was dying, because I didn't know for certain, although I had a pretty good idea. I couldn't bring myself to take away that last spark of hope. It can do wonders, and there's plenty in heaven and earth that we docs know nothing about. Simon knew he was being called to hear the heavenly chorus and had resolved things, as the terminally ill often do. They plan who and what they want and don't want to see and do; could be some old bloke they went to school with or religious problems that needed to be worked through.

'Your receptionist said that before her husband died last year she made him sign a heap of forms.'

'And it's a good thing she did,' I said. 'She saved herself a lot of trouble after.'

'Doc, you got anything you want me to sign?'

'No, Simon, I don't,' I said. 'I wish Wayne could be with you tonight.'

Simon smiled. 'That's okay, doc. His wife'll do. Remember I was telling you about somebody pilfering me bloody wood?'

'Yes.'

'Well, I finally got sick of it, so I got a detonator and put it in a log.'

I laughed.

'I then happened to go next door. Now Trev's a top bloke, doc. Me and him's mates. I never thought in a million years he would do that.'

'People do funny things.'

'You're not wrong. Now this piece of wood, it was unique. I picked it so I'd recognise it. I didn't want it going off in me own fireplace.'

We hit a pothole. 'Easy!' I cried to the driver, steadying my husband's friend.

'That log was sitting right there next to Trev's fireplace, where you stack up wood,' Simon continued. 'So I did a runner.'

'It must have done a substantial amount of damage.'

'Yeah, doc, it did,' he replied, with sad satisfaction. 'Trev never said nothing to me. And my wood pile hasn't shrunk since.'

We had a good laugh.

'I'll tell you something, if you promise not to tell anybody,' I said.

Simon's ears went up, like a dog. He always loved a good secret. 'Not a word, doc,' he said eagerly.

'Well, Wayne shot a stag not too long ago.' I thought Simon would rather hear one of Wayne's secrets than one of mine.

'Out of season,' he beamed. 'Ain't that just like him.'

'He and his mate were on a certain property. I won't say whose it is but you know it well. They got the word that Parks and Wildlife were checking vehicles for illicit game. They were a little bit nervous about how they were going to get it home.'

'No good leaving it there, doc.'

'That's exactly right. So Wayne got Jack to bring the ambulance up and they loaded the stag into the back. They had the lights flashing as they drove past the Parks and Wildlife checkpoint. They covered up the stag with a sheet, right where you're lying now. If they had pulled them up, it would have been interesting. But of course they weren't stopped and actually got a wave from the Wildlife officers.'

Simon laughed so hard he started coughing. Then he became quiet.

'What is it, Simon?' I asked. I knew he had something on his mind.

'I need to confess something, doc. I can't go to a priest. I'm what they call a lapsed Catholic. E-lapsed is more like it.'

'Try not to talk too much.'

'This can't wait.'

'Okay, then.'

'I been doing something ever since I was a boy, that I've never told nobody, not even me wife – especially me wife.'

'What's that, mate?'

Simon hesitated. I didn't say anything. After a while, Simon cleared his throat.

'I eat silverfish,' he said quietly.

I thought I'd heard it all, but patients constantly surprise you.

'I was eight and old Trev next door, he was nine,' Old Simon began. 'He dared me on me birthday to eat the first thing I saw moving around the house. He bet his fishing rod I was too much of a sook. I remembered that Mum always complained about insects eating her cookbook. I wanted to help, so I got me a nice big fat silverfish. I remember how fast it wiggled. I showed Trev, then I popped it in me mouth and swallowed. Trev waited for me to bring it back up, but I didn't. It tasted good. I started eating silverfish whenever I saw them. Then I started looking for them.'

Simon looked out the window, into the past. 'There's an art to eating silverfish,' he continued. 'To get the full flavour, you got to have at least ten big fat grandpas, still squirming. No good if they're dead. They dry out too quick. I never told nobody, but I don't want to go to me grave without somebody knowing.'

Somebody did know when Simon went to his Maker the next day. And somebody mourned.

He made their lives a misery

Dexter Veriform

'Gaol, yes gaol, my dear. Society's finally decided it does not approve, after all these years of upholding the attitudes it entrusted to me, such as life with dignity,' said Dexter Veriform. 'I've been thinking about endings,' he added, eyes full of betrayed trust. 'Painful, protracted, peaceful and assisted. We GPs are often present. People snicker about our theological pretensions, but sometimes we face situations that reinforce this attitude. Did I play God with Sandy MacSalter? He was bedbound and totally dependent. When he died it was a great relief.' The old family doctor leaned forward and tapped an arthritic forefinger on the filthy Perspex barrier separating us. 'I've tried to be responsive to my patients. One needed to talk about death. Another said nary a word. Sandy couldn't speak, poor little chap. Running through it all has been a canine chorus.' He tapped the barrier again, a hollow, defeated sound. 'Society's let me down badly.'

M R STEVENS rolled to a stop on the highway, leaned out of his old truck and asked, 'I'd put down Otis, doc, so why won't you treat me the same?' A border collie pricked his ears from the tray of the flatbed truck. He knew, we both knew, that his master had not been thriving for quite some time, since the old man's wife had died.

'Death's a normal biological process and we should let nature take its course,' I replied, continuing a discussion begun years ago. Leaning against the warmth of the car blunted the edge of the cold topic. What was Mr Stevens really asking? Was he afraid of losing control? Perhaps he just needed to know that the means were available should he choose that path. He was getting ready; the only thing he cared about was being at home at the end and allowed to go in his own time.

I'd just pulled over onto the side of the road, mesmerised at the end of a long day by the orange-and-magenta landscape created by the setting sun. My car looked like part of a toy train. I had to stop and get a grip. 'That's a lot more dignified than fighting off death at any cost,' I said, idly toeing the purple gravel, 'and I won't be pressured into doing what I believe is wrong.' Once, as an intern, a hospital nurse wanted me to kill an elderly woman who'd fallen and fractured her femur. I refused. I'm not a murderer. I went into medicine to save lives, not take them. First Do No Harm.

'I don't know doc,' he said. I liked Mr Stevens. He'd left school at the age of ten to tend the stock, yet I felt a stronger bond with him and his wife than with many of my colleagues. She was a wispy little thing from Scotland who could cook the pants off all my other patients combined. In the old days, Mrs Stevens whipped up a batch of scones whenever she saw me coming. She knew how partial I was to those hot, steaming little mounds. She had the touch, no doubt about it, possibly because she cooked so unbregrudgingly, with such love. 'Only take a minute, doc,' she'd say. 'No trouble at all.' She'd set out the jam of blackberries gathered from the thicket just outside town and freshly churned butter that didn't need to be refrigerated because her pantry was so cold, even in summer. I was simply another item to be set at the table for afternoon tea. We both missed her.

'The whole euthanasia debate focuses on one kind of pain, which is physical and usually cancer, for which we've got great relief,' I said, my words overpowered by a speeding log truck. So we wouldn't have to shout, I walked the few feet to his truck, once white, now caked with electric-pink dirt. Otis wagged his tail. 'What about spiritual and emotional pain?'

'Why stop with terminal physical illness, doc?' Mr Stevens persisted. The sun made us look as if we'd overdosed on carotene. 'Why not make euthanasia available to the dejected and the disabled and legalise it?'

'There's enough bureaucracy trying to control what we do already,' I said. 'For that reason alone I'd fight the legalisation process. And it's very personal, between a patient and his carer, and should remain that way. I personally would prefer not to be monitored by some pencil pusher with no field experience.'

'The thin end of the wedge,' the old man agreed.

'It may be fine in the first flush of bureaucratic passion, but what happens twenty years down the line when the agenda has changed? And change it will. It's the nature of bureaucrats to fiddle. Let's keep the whole thing informal and arbitrary,' I said, watching a red station wagon with Government plates overtake several vehicles at once.

'Those Government cars. Oughtta be a law,' Mr Stevens said, making moves to leave.

'Do patients realise that if the drugs don't work or don't work fast enough, their carers may smother them with a pillow or strangle them with their bare hands?' I said, stretching my back discreetly. I'm not as young as I used to be.

My patient shuddered.

'I can just imagine some young pup talking to a comatose elderly woman or emaciated AIDS patient,' I continued, warming to my subject. '"Now dear," he mimicked, "you're not dying fast enough, and I'm going on holiday and have a plane to catch, so even though we've brought forward your preferred date I'll still have to use the pillow. Bye bye. I'm off to the sun. Maybe I'll meet someone."'

I paused. Both of us had run out of steam.

'Oughtta watch that back, doc,' Mr Stevens said slowly.

He drove off. So did I.

I suppose I'm overly reflective these days, being locked away as I am. And for what? Doing what a patient wanted and what I knew to be right. Please forgive me. I've plenty of time to think in here, more than I want. What kind of care have I given over the years? Countless patients have asked for my help at the end. I've always done what I could, but not by holding a shotgun to anyone's head. Mine haven't asked that of me, thank God, at least until recently. Almost always it's extra morphine.

We GPs face endless ethical dilemmas daily. Is the life of a ten-year-old more valuable than that of an eighty-year-old? Should the family be told the entire truth? Should the patient? Thucydides Hare and I have discussed these matters exhaustively. What would Harey have done with my lone-wolf widower? Mr Stevens was in his late seventies. Soon after our roadside chat, we discovered a nasty carcinoma of the bowel. I could have locked him away, but as he refused treatment what was the point? He wasn't interested in palliative care. Why take the place of someone who genuinely wanted it, he asked? If he insisted on killing himself, I persuaded him to do so in the open where it would be easier to tidy up. Shooting yourself indoors or in a car is not to be encouraged. Somebody has to clean up the many bits and pieces. Mr Stevens shot himself by the incinerator, very tidily and thoughtfully. He left me that wonderful border collie.

That got me thinking about dogs I've encountered throughout my career, like the Great Dane in New Zealand who casually peed on my car window as I frantically cranked it up, praying it wouldn't jam. There was the spaniel pup our son took to cheer up Maggie Reid in the days after her multiple sclerosis was diagnosed.

And then there was Maloney. That was in Scotland, too, and a long time ago.

I always took my cocker spaniel round every fortnight to visit poor little Sandy MacSalter. He had been brain damaged at birth and lived with his family in a remote Highland village. Numerous children invariably tumbled out of their whitewashed croft and made a fuss.

'Can we no ge' a dog noo?' they kept badgering their parents.

'No, you've got to look after your brother upstairs,' came the weary reply. Mr MacSalter's job with the Forestry Commission kept them in mutton and milk, but did not stretch to spring lamb and cream. *Upstairs* was a dark little cubicle with just enough room for a bed. I always hoped the boy never understood the nature of his plight or surroundings.

The years passed. Maloney slowed down and the MacSalter children grew, including Sandy. His condition remained the same and he continued to be a tremendous burden on his family. His parents were very basic folks indeed and totally unequipped to handle their handicapped son. I'll give you an example of what I mean.

One winter Saturday, midnight approached. I nursed a last whisky at the schoolmaster's after a fine dinner, venison I think it was.

The phone went. That it was for me surprised no one.

'Yes, Fiona?' I asked the housekeeper.

'Mrs MacSalter Number Six has got a terrible backache and he wants you to go.' Mrs MacSalter Number Six, that's how people knew her throughout the area, to differentiate amongst the many families with the same surname.

He, not she.

'Right, well, I'll go.'

I didn't think it was urgent. I finished my drink, quite leisurely, said goodnight, got in the car and drove home. I took our housekeeper home and walked up to see Mrs MacSalter Number Six.

As soon as I entered the house, I heard the unmistakable sounds of second-stage labour coming from upstairs. This was the backache that *he* wanted me to attend.

'Why didn't you tell me she was in labour, mon?' I asked the husband.

'That's one thing she canna be,' he said with dead certainty.

I ran upstairs, following the screams.

'Mrs Mac,' I said to the woman on the bed, 'I've just got my ordinary bag with me. I've got to get my other bag. I'll be back as soon as I can. Try and hold on.'

Life's burdens had pounded the good woman's roundness, flattening her upper arms and throat. I don't think she heard a word I said. I ran home, phoned the midwife and ran back again, arriving just in time to field the baby as it shot out. I did the necessary. The baby was alright. The mother was not. Retained placenta. We sent her by ambulance to the nearest hospital, leaving chaos at the croft. All those children ran up and downstairs constantly, changing nappies or caring for their brother in some other way. Their father didn't know his knee from his elbow and got underfoot.

So there you have the very basic MacSalters. They weren't church-going people who could pray to their God and hope that suffering was good for the development of their souls. Unlike church organisations, they did not claim that GPs played God, nor did they murmur about the sanctity of life.

Another two babies later, poor Sandy contracted meningitis. 'I don't want to treat this child,' I thought, taking the thermometer from his mouth.

There are no easy answers. There's euthanasia and there's euthanasia. There's prophylactic euthanasia, involved euthanasia and non-consensual euthanasia, just for starters. Euthanasia may be prophylactic by acknowledging it to a patient as an option. The ensuing sense of control may render the act itself unnecessary. Some patients never do it, but keep moving the goalposts until they die naturally; and some survivors regret their attempt, like Mr McLean. By non-consensual, I mean the patient may be comatose and the family impatient, misguided or compassionate. Nothing like pressure from family members to galvanise an inexperienced doctor.

In the MacSalter case, the pressures were *on* the family, not *from* them.

I went downstairs to the kitchen. Sandy's father was just coming in the back door.

'Can we talk?' I asked.

Mrs MacSalter Number Six turned from the wood stove and nodded, her face in shadow in the late-afternoon gloom. She gestured for me to sit at the table. I did. Her husband went to the sink. My tone of voice told them something serious was afoot.

The noise level from all those children was something awesome. She stuck her head into the passageway and yelled for quiet. I reckoned we had about a minute and a half before the irrepressible youthful chorus resumed.

'It's Sandy,' I began.

They watched me.

'He's not going to get any better,' I said.

'Aye,' the forester replied.

'He's got meningitis. It's curable, if we give him antibiotics.

Or we could let nature take its course.'

She stared at the oven. He gazed into the depths of the sink. For a moment, no one spoke. Finally she asked, 'What do you think, doctor?'

'Sandy is eleven years old and able to swallow and that's about all,' I said. 'You focus your lives on him and he makes the lives of the other children a misery.'

They nodded. That was all.

I felt terrible.

No, there are no easy answers.

I was with the boy when he died. Some of his siblings were present. I said what I usually say over dead bodies and turned solemnly to the children. 'I'm very sorry to say that your brother has died.'

'Can we no ge' a dog noo,' was their only response.

Not long afterwards, Maloney had puppies. The MacSalter children got their dog. Lately I've been thinking about poor Sandy MacSalter and Mr McLean, the suicide with those eyes pleading with me to save him after he'd put a shotgun to his head. And pulled the trigger. So much love. So much pain. I hope I've helped. Who will help me out of this nightmare? What an insult to a career of caring! Will my wife bring in a little something if I ask her nicely?

Guilt by association

Thucydides Hare

*'Think about my home-visit stories,' Thucydides Hare said,
filling the second loaf pan. 'I've not hidden anything from you or
tried to paint myself in a good light. I've had doubts and my
wife's had difficult times all the way along, but we don't think of
it as hard. I'd be very wary of the Pollyanna attitude. All that
denial and repression may spawn an axe murderer in the family
somewhere.' He licked the spoon and the bowl. A bit of bright
beetroot batter nicked his nose as he scooped it into the two loaf
tins. 'I hesitate profoundly to wade into other people's marriages.
I can only say that Anna and I are more in love than ever.'
Harey positioned the tins in the centre of the oven and gently
closed the door. 'Now I must get back to work.' He breezed out,
cupboard doors open, the cyclone chef.*

I COULD NEVER summon any sympathy for Nellie Nyall,
the embezzling adulterer. Why not, I ask myself as a trained
medico. He'd presented very early in the piece with bad
nerves. I missed the connection between bad nerves and marital
problems. I prescribed a holiday. He certainly took my advice!

It began in medical school with Nellie's son, Canwell. One
would never meet a more decent chap than he. Canwell was a
few years ahead of me, so we weren't close, but everyone knew
everyone else and often each other's family members as well. We
all knew Nancy, Canwell's sister. She was a most well-bred young
lady, about my age and far beyond my reach. We appreciated her
charms nevertheless. Their mother, Marguerite, inherited one of
the minor fortunes of the day. And Nelson – ah, Nelson! Their
father reminded me of Muhammed Ali, an Albanian mercenary
who became the Ottoman viceroy of Egypt in 1805 despite

being illiterate until middle age.[12] As time went on, he taught himself to read and write – the Albanian adventurer, that is; Nellie always knew how to play the game.

Nellie was a medical adventurer pursuing a different kind of kingdom: one of the oldest hospitals in the city. Back then the concept of paying someone to administer a hospital was fairly novel. One of the most pervasive changes in the nature of medical practice since my father's time as a solo country GP in the 1920s and 1930s is the increasing complexity and cost, which begat bureaucrats to run the services. Even in my time as a medical student and hospital house officer in the late 1940s and early 1950s, we had just one part-time medical administrator who doubled as a surgical admitting officer in the casualty department. He did all the bookwork, supervised all equipment purchases and reported to the board once a month. The hospital had a thousand beds, a huge outpatient and casualty department turnover and several outpost hospitals, all run by this part-time man.

We respected Nellie – no mean feat in those days, let me tell you, as administrators were busy building reputations as interventionists, much to the annoyance of sincere GPs everywhere. Not Nellie. He left his doctors alone.

The medical press has covered the subject of third-party intervention in the doctor–patient relationship extensively. It's a highly charged subject, which it's almost impossible to get practising docs to think and talk about with detachment. Tension is unavoidable when that third party holds the purse strings.

Doctors in British-based health systems who whinge about government interference would really have something to complain about if they worked in US health maintenance organisations. Mangled care, not managed care, as they say. Private for-profit medical care organisations are far more oppressive than the NHS or, say, the Canadian system. And the paperwork. That's the last thing I want to see at the end of the day.

I thought – hoped – I'd left the cares of incipient interventionists far behind when I began my antipodean odyssey. Imagine my surprise when one beautiful autumn day the bank teller who served me was none other than the lovely sister of my medical school colleague.

'What are you doing here?' I asked with no great originality.

Nancy flashed me a sad smile. That a young lady of her class and age should be in this position, so far away from home, was indeed most irregular.

'Father,' she whispered, bowing her head. 'He embezzled quite a lot of money and disappeared with a secretary.'

'Oh Nancy, I *am* sorry,' I said, reaching across for her hand, a movement checked at once by the glares of the other tellers. In a bank, honest people do not allow their hands to cross the divide. 'How is Mrs Nyall?'

'Fortunately, the house was in Mother's name. She sold it as partial payment of the debt. We sold everything. Canwell dropped out of medical school. We came here to get away. We're trying to pay off the debt. Canwell's an ambulance driver. Mother works two part-time jobs. And I am here.'

Subsequently, I ran into Canwell at my golf club. He was also a member. We became reacquainted and the Nyalls became my patients. One day Canwell and I were walking to the eighteenth hole. It was a lovely day, with lush lawns and men in the distance looking like little white markers.

'Mother's not been feeling her best lately,' Canwell said, 'and I'm worried about her.'

'Have her come in and see me,' I said. We stopped walking and waited our turn.

'She denies that anything is wrong,' he said, 'but I know better. This business has been quite a strain for her.'

'I'll call in on my way home from work tomorrow.'

The Nyalls rented a small semi-detached accommodation in the least desirable part of town. Canwell had a bedroom to himself, as he was the man of the house. He provided moral leadership and did all the handyman-type stuff. Marguerite and Nancy shared the other bedroom.

I examined Marguerite and said, 'I suspect that you've had a mild myocardial infarction, unusual given your age and breeding, not so unusual considering the circumstances. You need to rest, Marguerite.'

'I can't risk losing my jobs.'

'It's either that or your health.'

Marguerite shook her head. I couldn't do a thing except admire her fortitude.

Then the influenza epidemic hit in 1957, the pandemic that lasted three or four weeks and caused many deaths, particularly amongst young people. One felt unwell in the morning, quite sick by the afternoon and died during the night. That rapidly progressing pneumonia and overwhelming poisoning of all the body systems was a nasty disease. People at high risk received a vaccine, including ambulance drivers such as Canwell. It didn't do him any good. The flu got him before it had time to work.

Nancy phoned at eight o'clock one morning. 'Sorry to ring you so early, doctor. It's Canwell. He's in bed with a very high temperature. Can you come and see him?' No mistaking that pleading, desperate tone.

'Of course,' I said, gulping the last of my breakfast tea. 'I'm on my way.'

Canwell was obviously very ill. 'There's not much I can do, I'm afraid,' I said to his mother and sister. 'We'll pump in as much antibiotic as we can.' I gave him penicillin and put him on another antibiotic, Aureomycin. Big capsules.

'I'll come back later,' I said.

At about eleven, one look told me what I dreaded: Canwell had deteriorated. His temperature was higher, his breathing much worse. 'We'd better get him to the hospital,' I told Marguerite and Nancy, both of whom had stayed home from work. 'Can one of you ring the ambulance?'

'I want to go in a taxi,' Canwell protested.

'No way, mate. You're going in an ambulance.'

At the hospital, we hit my doomed friend with every antibiotic in the book, mainly penicillin, streptomycin and Aureomycin. We included steroids in the two intravenous cocktails we gave him, one in each arm. Poor Canwell couldn't take anything by mouth at that stage. He had something akin to Waterhouse–Friedrickson syndrome, a total shutdown of vital endocrine glands that can happen with overwhelming toxaemia; that's why we gave him steroids.

I saw Canwell again after lunch. He had so deteriorated that I called in a colleague, a specialist in internal medicine.

'I hope these massive doses of streptomycin won't make him deaf,' I said, 'or maybe it's only long-term use that does that, as with TB.'

My colleague shook his head and said softly, 'You needn't worry about deafness.'

I stayed with Canwell as much as I could. I had many patients to see and a huge number of home visits. He lived through the night but died about six o'clock the next morning. It was a devastating experience for all of us.

The story didn't end there. Two other elements comprised my moment of truth, and they happened on the same day. About a month later Marguerite came in to see me, a bit short of breath.

'How are you feeling?' I began, assuming she'd come about her heart.

'Well, thank you, doctor, that's not why I came,' she said with such considerable dignity that I got angry anew with her ex-husband.

Back when I was a house officer, I'd missed Nellie's signals. This triggered an interest in social medicine. Later, in an epidemiological trial, I interviewed one hundred and four randomly selected GPs in three large industrial towns in the north of England. Among my questions – designed to probe perceptions – I requested they estimate the proportion of patients who presented with 'trivial complaints.' Almost half gave me a figure from one to ninety-nine percent. The rest answered completely differently, saying in effect, 'So far as the patient is concerned, nothing's trivial.' I think the GPs in the latter group had clearer insight into the reality of what is now fashionably called holistic medicine. They understood the relationship between 'bad nerves' and 'marital problems' better than those who saw 'hundreds' of patients with 'bad nerves' but rarely those with marital problems.

'Are you sure, Marguerite?' I asked. 'You're a bit breathless.'

She nodded and reached into her handbag. 'I want to pay for the visits you made to Canwell.'

SECRETS FROM THE BLACK BAG

'No, please, Marguerite, that's not necessary. He was my friend.'

'He was covered by insurance and I'll get it back,' she insisted, eyes tearing. 'I want to pay for the services you provided. Nancy and I are very grateful. We realise you did everything you could.'

'That blasted epidemic singled out the nicest people,' I grunted, swallowing hard.

That evening, the partners held the monthly meeting. I'd joined that exalted rank after my marriage earlier in the year. The eleven partners reviewed the month's takings at these meetings. I found this one particularly obscene. They rubbed their hands in glee at the huge amounts of money that influenza had generated. The money came not only from patients but also from our comprehensive health insurance program. All of us had been frantically busy. It was the best month the practice ever recorded, said a partner I'd never liked. Some of his patients had died, including a young nurse at a community hospital, a most capable girl whom we all loved. As I looked at his smooth face unafflicted by strong emotion, I wondered whether he'd already collected his fees from the girl's family. He palmed his fees like a magician and preferred payment in cash, for which he did not always issue receipts.

No sleight of hand could erase from my mind's eye visions of Canwell Nyall's face and those of his poor mother and sister. I thought, That's it – there's no way I can go on practising medicine with this lot or in this context. I'd bottled up most of my feelings until then.

Someone asked, 'Should we consider hiring an administrator?'

I jumped up, knocking over my chair, and cried, 'Greedy bastards! Preventing people from getting sick in the first place is far nobler than waiting for them to fall ill and trying to help them and then gloating when they die.'

I knew they all had wives and families who required care and tending.

All the same.

'I've had enough,' I said, and stormed out. Anna would understand. I started my studies in epidemiology shortly thereafter.

The partners had their wives, I had Anna and poor Marguerite still had the burdensome memory of Nellie. Marriage through the ages, a litany of bad nerves and funny turns. More like a death sentence sometimes than a prescription for eternal bliss.

Cherchez la femme

Noose Grimely

Noose Grimely reached into his desk. 'Something within me stirs in the windless weather of midday, which Bulfinch called the time of sunstrokes and siesta-nightmares,' he said. He pulled out a bottle and poured himself a whisky. 'All that putting up with it, smoothing things over, putting on a brave face, running on empty, leaving what's just below the surface to fester and gnarl. What do I have to look forward to? A lifetime of nurturing nasty little secrets, mine, hers and ours, a family of half-lit candles that sputter and snuff no matter how fiercely I nurture them. How could she?'

J AN LUYDIK HAUNTS ME. If he's honest, every doctor will admit to such a patient. Jan's one of the reasons I want to leave general practice. I'll never forget that elderly Dutchman whom I regard as a late casualty of the Second World War, a sufferer from post-traumatic stress disorder. He liked to come in and talk and I listened. At least I tried to. Most of the time.

'Something funny's wrong with my legs, Dr Grimely,' Jan said one day, so softly I could barely hear him. Nothing seemed to be wrong, although he was shuffling a bit more than usual. I wondered about depression. Many depressed people think something's physically wrong.

'How's your appetite, Jan?'

'Well, I *am* a bit off my food, Dr Grimely,' he replied, brushing his thick white hair off a broad red nose. This should have alerted me. Meals were a great pleasure for him.

'Do you ever think about suicide, Jan?'

'Sometimes,' came the whispered reply. Using Zoltan Nagy's retrospectoscope, I know now he wanted me to dissuade him. At the time, I was going through a phase of, If that's your decision, I respect it. I didn't try to persuade him otherwise, to my everlasting regret.

Jan left Europe as a young man looking for a better life. I could relate to that. I'd done some living before I met my wife. I did psychiatry in Canada and worked as a psychiatric registrar in a hospital. My lady friend and I broke up, which propelled me home. *Cherchez la femme*. Blame the woman. Something must be wrong with me because this relationship did not work. I planned to earn enough money for psychoanalysis, which would fix me up. Then I'd go back to Canada. I found work as a psychiatric registrar in a mental hospital here, went through Jungian analysis and met my wife. I never returned to Canada. *Cherchez la bloody femme*.

Jan met his wife here one spring day when he stopped to fill his car with petrol. Her father owned the local garage. Jan married the business. His wife died from a stroke several years before I knew him. He missed her terribly.

Shortly thereafter a winter flu epidemic struck. I got busy with other patients and forgot about Jan.

One day a neighbour came banging on the door. 'It's Jan!'

I went immediately, with a sense of foreboding. Jan lay on the linoleum surrounded by blood, a hole in the top of his head and a hole in the ceiling. He shot himself with a twenty-two. Fawn-coloured linoleum with brown speckles in a nobbled pattern is quite common in older houses round here. This job lot of lino must have been cheap and plentiful enough to do most of the houses in the state. I think of Jan Luydik and his blood-splattered floor and ceiling whenever I see this linoleum.

I should have acted differently, but the alternative would have been to send Jan to a psychiatric hospital and perhaps give him ECT. How much good would it have done to give him the volts? I feel responsible. There's a tendency to blame yourself if someone close to you dies, patient or not. You feel you've done the wrong thing or not done the right thing. You have to live with it. How many others have I sent to their deaths through my incompetence or insensitivity?

Jan Luydik haunts me. I don't attempt to justify it, and I know I should refuse to feel guilty about somebody else's behaviour. How much guilt can we as GPs realistically carry? If you felt guilty for every failure and mistake, you'd be of no use to anyone. Perhaps I am of no use to anyone.

Magic pills and pumps

Yam Peale

*'You ask if I'll go back,' Yam Peale said, pushing aside a cascade
of weeds to read an old inscription on a tombstone. 'We were
there last year, but I doubt that we'll return. I'd go tomorrow but
Centuria doesn't want to, and I think the children need me more
than they did when they were young. Not only that, but last time
we were there I felt a bit used. There were a number of other
doctors, a few of them local, who didn't do their share of after-
hours work. They simply left and could not be found, so I had to
do it all. It was quite tiring. Centy was incensed by the injustice
and ingratitude – although we learned long ago that those
concepts have cultural overlays.*

DOCTOR, DOCTOR,' a cultured English voice called
urgently. As I emerged into consciousness, I realised
that the woman stood leaning over the foot of the bed
and was getting closer. Centuria sighed beside me.

Things could be worse. That is a Buddhist tenet made sim-
plistic. Considering the sufferings of others gives perspective to
one's own. For example, a home visit wrenches a husband from
the arms of his wife in the middle of the night. What could be
worse? I'll tell you: a patient who walks into your bedroom at
three o'clock in the morning.

'Doctor, doctor.' The more conscious I became, the louder the
voice got.

Streams of visitors seeking medical help, some urgent, some
not so urgent, occupied my weekends. The lack of privacy was a
difficult trial. God had sent me to work in a community with a
singular sense of space and mode of communication. The West
African telephone system was so poor that most people came to

the doctor's house if they needed help. They were busy during the day so they went on weekends. I had no time off unless I physically left town. I did a lot of that when I'd have preferred to potter around the house with Centy and the children, but you never knew when half a dozen patients would walk into your lounge and sit down.

'Doctor, doctor.'

I'd forgotten to lock the front door. We lived in a house in a large compound, within which were various residential complexes made of concrete blocks. They were well-constructed, three-bedroom homes, well plumbed and wired and topped by corrugated iron roofs. The church had constructed six family homes and a number of units for couples and single people in the compound, which accommodated both local and expatriate staff.

'It's my father, doctor.'

'What happened?'

'He's been vomiting blood.'

I sent the hospital ambulance for him. A bleeding ulcer necessitated a drive to his village in the distant volcanic hills. I despatched his daughter and calculated that I could sleep for some hours before the ambulance arrived.

As I tried to get back to sleep, thoughts swirled through my mind about different cultures. As I've got older I've come to appreciate other religions. I was a bit intolerant in my youth I'm afraid, like that time I obliterated a magic circle drawn in the dirt to prove that nothing would happen to the horrified villagers.

A spiritual dimension has always been important to my practice. I occasionally raise the subject with receptive patients. I'm not talking only about Christianity or other Western religions. Eastern religions interest me, particularly Buddhism with its emphasis on balance between material and spiritual progress. We can achieve this through love and compassion, the essence of all religions.

Centy rolled over in her sleep, the perfect wife. I sympathised with those medical wives who gained reputations as dragon ladies. They had to protect their husbands. The style of one neighbour in our compound encouraged dropping in. His wife held the opposite view, so people felt that you'd be alright if you could get round this guy's wife.

I couldn't get back to sleep after being awakened by the worried daughter. Just as well, because Mrs CJ Momotole sailed in a short while later. She exemplified the average patient there: middle-aged with a sore tummy. They all had *ciwo ciki*, pronounced *chew-on-chicky*, the household name for abdominal pain. It could mean anything. *Ciwo* was the Hausa word for illness, sickness or pain. *Ciki* meant abdomen. They added an 'n' to make it a genitive. If somebody had *ciki*, it meant she was pregnant. Where do you start to sort them out? You go through all the questions we learned as medical students. Where is it located? Does it radiate? What does it feel like? What time of the day does it come on? Often you don't get much information. Even now, when patients in the West complain of abdominal pain, I shudder and think of all the possibilities.

Mrs Momotole appeared at my bedroom door with a man in tow. She wore a traditional embroidered wrapper called a *zane*, pronounced *zanay*, and a tie around her head, which she tucked in. This respectable dress announced her relative wealth. Like most women there, she'd had her ears pierced. She wore a necklace and bracelets made out of circular tube grasses, a local material. Wealthier women bought Western-style jewellery from the market. She was quite clean and average weight, unlike her poorer, skinny countrywomen. They could be quite heavy in other parts of the country where female obesity was acceptable, even desirable.

I led the patient and translator into the lounge and turned on the light, moving and speaking quietly so as not to awaken the children.

Examination revealed little. Why couldn't she come tomorrow during office hours to the hospital, where I had all my equipment? The translator replied, 'Doctor, no need to do all that, just scribble prescription for anything, doesn't matter, just as long as they've seen the white doctor they'll be happy.'

'Well don't you think I should at least lay hands on them?' I whispered to the man.

'Oh yes yes, that's important.'

I had trained to practise medicine differently. Ideally I'd pay much more attention to the history. I examined the woman before me to rule out obvious things. Often, they had parasites and big livers and spleens from schistosomiasis, that sort of thing. Sometimes you could feel abdominal TB. 'Do you have bowel problems?' I asked.

'No.'

'Blood and mucus in the stool?' I was looking for anything to suggest worm infestation or amoebiasis.

'No.'

'Have you been vomiting?' I wonder about jaundice.

'No.'

As if I needed reminding that it was four-thirty in the morning, the Muslim prayer call thundered through various loudspeakers scattered around the town, loud enough to wake the dead.

As soon as the prayer call ceased I examined Mrs Momotole's belly for a fibroid uterus. 'Bleeding?' I asked. Perhaps a gynaecological problem.

'No.'

'Weight loss?'

'No.'

'Discomfort in this area? A general feeling of being unwell, a dragging feeling?'

'No, no, no.'

Primary cancer of the liver was quite common there, particularly amongst men. Even the younger men got it. They might complain of a mass or weight loss. When you examined them, there it was: liver enlargement. It has a typical feel, but you can't always rule out other causes. If they had the typical appearance, had lost a lot of weight, really looked terminal, were anaemic and had an enlarged liver, then the diagnosis was obvious. We didn't always biopsy them, as it sometimes caused bleeding and hastened their demise. And there was no treatment. Here it occurs in people with cirrhosis of the liver, although the most common cause is Hepatitis B. Over there it's probably all due to the prevalence of

Hepatitis B in the community. A few million dollars well invested could see an immunisation programme that would eradicate this problem, but the logistics are mind-boggling.

I wrote a prescription for PCM. Paracetamol. They loved those little abbreviations. TCN was tetracycline. There was a list as long as your arm. I didn't think she had worms, so a broad-spectrum anti-worm medication such as Verlox would have been useless. I suspected a fibroid uterus, not something that I could have done much about at that point. I also gave her a prescription for Vitamin B complex, a popular placebo. Patients liked to walk away with a prescription. They didn't mind paying for it, otherwise they didn't consider it valuable. The middle-aged woman left happy. I'd given her what she wanted.

What I'd given Mrs CJ Momotole wouldn't keep her happy for long. That's the nature of suffering. Had I missed anything, I wondered as I drifted off for a few hours' sleep after the woman's departure. Her suffering was just as real as that of the villager vomiting blood.

Later that day, I would encounter a third form of suffering entirely different from ulcers and *ciwo ciki*. I'd be miscommunicating in three languages through two translators about a very sensitive male condition.

I supervised approximately two hundred clinics around the country. I saw the purpose of these visits as teaching and encouraging the staff and inspecting the facilities. The staff and local people thought otherwise. A doctor's visit presented an opportunity for medical consultations – understandable, considering that some of these villages had never had a doctor visit them. I tried to discourage excessive numbers of patients but couldn't refuse to see them.

Later that morning we drove to a Yoruba-speaking village. There were no urgent bedside whisperings. Quite the contrary. Ignoring my specific instructions for a discreet arrival, a loud voice pierced the din. From the car window, I saw a young boy in light-coloured trousers and a cotton long-sleeved business shirt, somewhat dilapidated, with the tail hanging out.

'Come! Come one and all!' he proclaimed in the local language. 'All those with illnesses or medical complaints of any kind!

The white doctor has come!' His thongs flapped as he walked. 'Come and see him! Come! Come now!'

Already over seventy patients waited outside and I only had a couple of hours before I had to leave.

The town crier announced my visit in church and marketplace. Our arrival was something splendid, after ten hours in an old transport van without air-conditioning on a hot, dusty day over pitted, bumpy roads. The district supervisor accompanied us. He'd been the village health worker for many years, so people lined the streets as for a visit by the Queen. They welcomed him and he waved back, enjoying every minute of his celebrity. Of secondary importance were the van's supplies and skilled professionals, such as a wonderfully good-natured American missionary nurse.

I greeted the staff before undertaking a detailed tour of the clinic to check cleanliness and adequacy of supplies and records. The small building's location on the outskirts of town made it accessible to the numerous nearby villages. A church compound housed the clinic. The pastor's house was the closest building, a reasonable quality concrete-block house. The typical villager lived in a mud brick dwelling with a corrugated iron or tin roof, if it was closer to the city, or a traditional thatched roof if farther away. Like most of the clinics, this one was mud brick.

The agreeable nurse provided much needed spiritual support. We were close to the Benin border and I had no intention of crossing over. Benin had grown fat on the slave trade in the sixteenth-to-nineteenth centuries, first with the Portuguese, then with the British and French. Border skirmishes occurred frequently. I worried I'd be caught in crossfire or taken by Beninois as a twentieth-century medical slave.

The blasted red dust that settled on me like a second skin superseded thoughts of medical slavery and personal privacy. The local health worker kindly carried water for us to wash, which he hauled up a flight of stairs, as the clinic perched on quite a high foundation. A major injury had left this man, the Yoruba-to-English interpreter, with a deformed face and several missing teeth. I didn't speak Yoruba beyond a few greetings and many of the patients didn't speak English. Another health worker translated from the local language to Yoruba. This process rapidly became tedious, especially on matters of a delicate nature.

Doctor–patient miscommunication in several languages about a personal, private medical condition seemed inevitable.

'Next, please,' I said.

In strode Mr Natatingou, a senior man of substance from one of hundreds of tribal groups through the middle belt, as they called it, not the true north. Unlike the average elderly rural male patient, Mr Natatingou wore slip-on shoes, a *hoola*, or hat, and a set of trousers under a flowing pink *riga*, or gown, with an embroidered neck. The quality of clothing deteriorated as people got poorer, although they always looked nice. Dress and appearance were a significant part of that culture.

'What's wrong?' I asked Mr Natatingou via the two interpreters.

'Impotence,' they said.

Many elderly *el-hajis* had four wives, so it was common for fifty- or sixty-year-old men to complain that they couldn't perform the way they did thirty years ago. If he was able to have intercourse only once a night, he felt that he had a major problem. I had to ask some fairly personal and detailed questions about the nature of Mr Natatingou's impotence. Was it complete? Was he ever able to have an erection? Did he get erections on some occasions and not on others? The former indicated a physical cause, the latter psychological. Impotence can be a difficult problem to assess, explain and treat in any setting; I found doing it in another culture through two interpreters challenging indeed. Nevertheless, I struggled on for some time.

'How is your general health?'

'Fine.'

I measured his blood pressure. Easy. I had to determine whether Mr Natatingou's impotence was due to diabetes, spinal cord damage or other organic causes. As we had no urine sticks, I asked, 'Do ants like to drink your urine?' I'd have loved to know how that one reached him.

Mr Natatingou looked at me quizzically and shook his head. Had he understood the question? Perhaps I should press on and inquire about white stains on black shoes, made by sugar crystals as the urine dries. Few people I encountered wore black shoes, which red dust would soon cover. Physical examination revealed no neurological cause for Mr Natatingou's condition. I didn't have the biomedical back-up to test for kidney or liver failure and other organic diseases. The language barrier made careful history-taking impossible. Organic causes were far less common than psychological ones or aging. How could I determine psychological causes, how could I really listen to the patient and his partner or partners with the Third Ear?

I determined that Mr Natatingou was probably slowing down with age. It was the Buddhist principle of the suffering of old age. I tried to reassure him and, through the translators, to teach him techniques such as defusing the focus on having erections and setting up non-intercourse situations. I knew a lot of Western counselling techniques that were supposed to work, but I don't think I ever implemented them successfully even in my own country. Men have got their pride. How do you transfer that to another culture? You could make a case for forgetting about it entirely, because you're probably not going to achieve anything anyway.

'What about Dr Fletcher's machine?'

Ah. So this was why he had come. As happens, we got to the real reason for his visit rather late in the piece.

An American urologist had recently arrived with a few artificial vacuum devices for impotence. He loaned two out and lost them in no time. Word spread rapidly.

'I'm afraid they're only available from the US,' I said.

'Give me an address. I'll pay anything,' Mr Natatingou said through the translators. He adjusted his *riga* with dignity.

No wonder the US has such an amazing reputation.

My counselling efforts failed abysmally. Who knows what Mr Natatingou heard? I'd like to ask him, 'What did that doctor say to you?' You know it's not going to do much good, but men come with a problem, you're a doctor and they need advice. In the end, they'll thank you and it probably won't make any difference, but the perception is that you tried to help.

After we finished the formal consultation, we discovered quite by accident that Hausa was Mr Natatingou's mother tongue – in which I was fluent! After all that, we switched to Hausa and had a relaxed and communicative discussion about his problem. Nevertheless, I'm sure Mr Natatingou is still impotent. Things could be worse.

And yes, we always remembered to lock the door at night.

'Nothing agrees with me, doctor'

Zoltan Nagy

'You must do battle in your own war, pet,' Zoltan Nagy said, kissing one cheek, then the other with hard dry pecks that smelled of pfeffernusse, gardenia and mint julep. 'Go. I send you forth. Your old friend needs to be alone, to fortify himself to see overexposed slides in faraway places with the heads cut off. Ah, the medical fraternity! I do not know which is more tedious: Dr Peale's missionary zeal or Professor Hare's ethical superiority. To help me decide, I shall open a cognac bottled when Dostoyevsky was writing The Idiot. *Thank you no, I can judge the vintage by myself. I shall probably hear about miracles. Did I tell you that one of my patients experienced that happy event? Never underestimate the power of hope, pet.'*

W E HAD ALL GIVEN UP on the wheelchair-bound Mrs Seligman, and then the electric meter reader cured her. Perhaps I had better explain. I will start with some background on patients like her.

Some patients need to feel superior, or equal, which may involve withholding information. That self-deception may endanger their health. They play a game with their doctors called Side Effects, or Nothing Agrees with Me, Doctor. Whatever you give them, they get throbbing here and something else there. It is always the same. They come back to you and say, 'I couldn't take your tablets, doctor.' The *your* is significant. It is not the tablets, it is *your* tablets. They are infuriating, because they are just proving a point. Psychiatrists claim they are saying, 'Father was wrong and you are trying to be my father so I am going to prove you wrong.'

A primitive way exists to beat them at this game. These patients work on the assumption that the doctor is always wrong. When they list their symptoms you say, 'Right, I am giving you these tablets. I should warn you they may cause a rash, you may start to tremble, you will probably feel sick and get a dreadful headache. If you persevere, you will be alright.' Either they get the side effects you were right about or they do not get any side effects and they get better, about which you were also right. It is a cruel trick to play, but there you are.

Doctors play other games with patients, although perhaps not deliberately. Miss B comes in with a pain. She is obese so you say to her, 'You will never get rid of that pain unless you lose weight,' knowing full well the poor woman cannot lose weight. You have won. Her pain is not your fault anymore. Patients with chronic, unfixable pain we write off as psychological. It is a peculiar paradigm. We doctors sometimes feel, 'If you do not get better when I tell you to, you must be a nut.' Circumstances have proved us wrong so often that many have relinquished these thoughts, although some surgeons still think, 'If my operation did not work, it is your fault.'

As for Mrs Seligman, I saw her on my rounds. I will not tell you what we thought of her. She had chronic back pain and sensitivity to drugs. I took her over from my senior partner, who shook his head tellingly over whisky one night many years ago. Whatever he prescribed made her tummy throb. Nothing fixed her back. This pained us. The nice Mrs Seligman had deteriorated so badly by the time I inherited her as to be completely wheelchair-bound. It took a large man to lift her between her bed and her wheelchair.

I visited Mrs Seligman regularly for another prescription and a chat. Nothing else could be done. I went infrequently, as her village lay on the periphery of our practice. Natives of deepest suburbia and commuters from London inhabited this village. Many worked for the BBC or the Foreign Office, providing two different social strata. Mrs Seligman's husband had worked with the latter during the War, at something mysterious that assured his widow a permanent, substantial pension. No one knew for certain she *was* a widow. Mr Seligman departed the village in a most singular fashion late one night, never to return. The distraught woman claimed he had succumbed to a potentially contagious tropical disease. This was too far outside the experience of most of the villagers, who whispered about Another Woman. The old deaconess next door insisted she heard a fusillade and saw Mr Seligman run out holding his bottom, which was peppered with holes.

One day I called in just before lunch. Mrs Seligman was not about, so I sat in the parlour, waiting for her to wheel herself in. She no longer looked like the champion winner of every available sharp-shooting award, with her eyes round as targets and sweet fleshy cheeks.

In the midst of my desultory examination of the marksmanship trophies above the fireplace, in she came.

I could not believe my eyes. 'What on *earth* has happened to you?'

Mrs Seligman walked through the door, *walked*, not wheeled. 'The man came to read the electric meter,' she explained. 'It's in the cupboard under the stairs. I wheeled myself to the front door and let him in.'

'What did he do, perform voodoo?'

Mrs Seligman smiled and shook her head. 'I led him to the cupboard and opened it. Somehow my wheelchair flipped forward and tossed me out on my head.'

At the thought of possible head injury, I jumped up to examine her.

'No need, doctor,' she said. 'As the meter man tried to help me up, I somehow got my feet.'

'You mean you walked?'

'Yes.'

I do not know if throwing people out of wheelchairs onto their heads is good treatment for the paralysed, but it worked for Mrs Seligman. I can only think she suffered from some sort of chronic misalignment. Maybe there *is* something in chiropractics after all. Or perhaps hysterical paralysis had outlived its usefulness.

Mrs Seligman not only walked, she never needed a wheelchair again. Perhaps there is a lesson to be learned. Ought I to have acted differently? Should we GPs keep experimenting until our difficult patients say, 'That agrees with me, doctor?'

How much good do we do? Eight hundred years ago, Petrarch deplored medical arrogance and learned theories. He insisted that the company of friends was the best prescription for the preservation and restoration of health. He had four medical friends whom he admitted only as friends in times of illness. Have I made much difference in people's lives? I was not much use to Mrs Seligman. She received better medical service from the electric meter reader.

An old soldier's last bullet

Hugh Page-Russell

*'Fetch that phallic torch from the shelf. I'll buy it for you,' said
Hugh Page-Russell. 'Help you to see in the dark. Blackouts.' We
waited behind a man in an old navy coat with an armful of
magazines served by a slow-moving cashier. Dr Page-Russell eyed
the man for a moment and said, 'Had a patient once. Returned
soldier. Like me. Adored his wife. They fought like cat and dog.'
Our turn came. We laid the torch on the counter, next to the
battery-operated wonders of modern technology. 'Things got out of
control one day. Had to leave a waiting room. Full of patients,
drug reps, community workers.'*

I HAVE ONE BULLET LEFT,' Mr Rice said on the telephone.
He was a returned soldier in his late sixties saddled with a
hag. He never had kids. Like me. Far as I know. He lived one
hundred and four yards from the surgery. Wife was arguing with
him. Locked herself in the bathroom. His voice on the phone
told me all I needed to know. 'So I said to her, "If that's how you
feel, that life's not worth living, I might as well put you out of
your misery".'

'Mr Rice, you can't–'

'So I got my gun out of the cupboard and tried to shoot her.'

'She hurt badly?'

'Naw, I missed, on purpose,' he grunted. 'Haven't seen her
move that fast in years.'

'Why'd you call me?'

'I have one bullet left and I'm keeping it for myself,' he said.
'What are you going to do about it?'

'Coming over immediately. Wait.'

'Call police,' I shouted at the receptionist as I sped out the door.

Did the one-hundred-yard dash from the surgery to Mr Rice's house quick-smart. Banged at an old front door. Peeling paint.

No answer. Let myself in. 'Mr Rice,' I called. 'Dr Page-Russell here.'

'You alone?' came a voice from the end of the hall.

'Yes.'

'How do I know that?'

'Open the door.'

A door cracked. No one exited. I shot down the hall.

'In here.' The voice sounded closer.

Followed it to the sitting room. Saw the same rug covering the same threadbare spot on the same carpet.

'I've lived too long,' the elderly man said. Hate to hear that weary tone and see the jacket and the droop of his head, as care-worn as the room not decorated since World War II.

'Give me that twenty-two. We'll talk.' Faint sounds at the front door. Hoped it was police.

'No,' he said. 'You can talk, but I'm keeping the gun.'

'You might shoot me.'

'The bullet's for me, doc,' Mr Rice said again.

'Show me.'

Mr Rice opened the barrel. Handed me the only bullet. I hoped. He handled the weapon comfortably, from long experience. Here was one World War II veteran who hadn't talked about wartime experiences.

'Mr Rice.'

'How can she say that life's not worth living, doc?'

'Her way of seeking attention.'

'I killed close-up – men whose faces I still see – and watched my own men die, for *her*, doc. Thinking of her got me through the war.'

'You're having a bad day, Mr Rice.'

'I've lived too long,' he repeated bitterly.

'Happens to all of us.'

'Even you?'

'Especially. Perhaps those new tablets we put you on–'

'To hell with your damn tablets,' he replied. He grabbed the bullet from me and knocked it back into its chamber.

'What happened during the war?' I asked. Hoped I wasn't opening a Pandora's box I couldn't close.

Mr Rice's face got that haunted look seen on the faces of concentration camp survivors. 'My father's elder brother died unexpectedly in England, without a will,' he explained. 'I had to go over and sort out his affairs. I hated to leave Judith' – he gestured with the twenty-two towards the bathroom – 'and we were just engaged, but Dad was too ill to travel.'

'That was brave, with war looming.'

'I had to go, for Dad. I got caught in it and drafted, and then came one long nightmare after another. I ended up on the Rhine, in charge of a boat – don't ask me how. I led my men to their deaths. I thought I knew what I was doing, but it still haunts me.'

'No absolutes. In colonial times, doctors were magistrates. Attended floggings.'

'What do you mean?'

'There's been publicity lately of doctors involved in torture. If our culture forced doctors to attend torture cases, ninety-nine percent would. If we didn't we'd be tortured ourselves. Or our families would. What happened that night?'

'We were supposed to try to cross the Rhine, with the Germans sitting there, waiting for us. We killed some of them and they killed most of us. Only one of my men survived. We kept in touch for a while, but we had nothing in common except that mass slaughter. You know, doc, I think about my men every day. All twenty-five of them. I pray for them by name. I can still see them as clearly as I see you. And she' – another derisory gesture – 'tells me life isn't worth living.' He points the twenty-two towards the bathroom. 'How dare she.'

'Talk to the missus?'

'I used to, but she got that bored look on her face so I stopped. War bore. She never noticed my silence, or maybe she did. I never mentioned it to her again. Before long I wasn't telling anybody.'

The police came. I'd engaged the old veteran so that he could be overpowered easily. Police took the gun. They did not press charges. Thankfully.

Started out the door, to work. Detoured to the bathroom. Tapped and said, 'You can come out, Mrs Rice.' Wanted to say a lot more, but I had to get back. 'Ring and make an appointment, Mrs Rice. Let's prevent a repetition of this.'

She never rang.

He had my sympathy. Two old soldiers.

The honourable thief

Amaranth Fillet/Zoltan Nagy

*'Once when I was a wild teenager, Uncle Zoltan – you've met Dr
Nagy, I believe – tried to sort me out by taking me on a home
visit with him,' said Amaranth Fillet. The sounds of Tutti Frutti
blasted from the speakers on the veranda. 'It was the first one I
ever did, and I wasn't even a medical student. I've never forgotten
Olyce Parp. He liked Little Richard. At that stage, I was
uncontrollable. Mr Parp liked that too. Here,' she said, reaching
into a recess near the left speaker. 'I want to give you this. Just a
pebble, small and black. Olyce took it from his Japanese couple.
He gave it to me long ago. For the quest. I'm passing it on to you.
Wooo-ooo-ooo … '*

WHAT OLYCE PARP hated most about police involvement in his life was the noise, the clunk of cell doors,
the abrasive speech and the bells and buzzers that
clanged away his life in segments. Olyce Parp accepted police in
his professional life as an occupational hazard – after all, he *was*
a thief – but his private life, well, that was something else. Olyce
and I had a lot in common. We both chose professions requiring
secrecy. My fuse is shortening regarding home visits as I grow
older. So did Olyce's. The Parps lived on charity from the
Salvation Army and the City Mission. Not for them what AJ
Cronin called the sublime fortitude of the very poor.[13]

Unfortunately the Parps, by their sheer numbers, needed
more of everything. Olyce provided it by following the local profession of inefficient low-level thieving. He stole cigarettes from
warehouses and tyres from service stations. The televisions he
took from people's homes were heavier in those days, but Olyce
was strong. Often he ended up in gaol.

Which is where he and Uncle Zoltan first met. Uncle Z had gone one night to retrieve Olyce's cellmate, whose driving manners deteriorated when he drank. Olyce observed that Uncle Z's accent was identical to his grandfather's, who had come to the antipodes to make his fortune after disgracing the family back home. This gave birth to a doctor–patient bond I'll never forget.

Also emblazoned on my mind is the loving wife. Wheezing from sheer bulk, the distressed woman now led me to their sleeping alcove. 'It's his bronco-itis, doctor,' Mrs P explained, conjuring up images of black stallions galloping across silver plains of sage. 'Bad this time, real bad.'

They say a woman stands behind every good man – or leans, as Mrs Parp did that time I saw Olyce. Actually, we were both leaning out the window, watching Uncle Zoltan's car surrounded by all the children in the neighbourhood.

'Will there be any tyres left when we've finished?' I wondered.

'If anybody damages my car I won't come here again,' Uncle Zoltan said sternly to Mrs Parp.

That good lady, all bosom and heavy breathing, let forth a verbal stream that would make most sergeant majors blush, in a voice like Aretha Franklin. R-E-S-P-E-C-T. The children scattered like buckshot.

'You're the only person who can park a Mercedes round here, doctor, without having the body scratched or worse,' she said.

She led us to the patient. Uncle Z leaned forward for the examination. Mrs Parp held a candle over the three of them, forming the protective apex of a lumpy triangle reminiscent of a cold, dark Dutch Masters painting. A drift of smoke from the fire sliced the room in two like the layers of a torte. I bent closer to catch Olyce's whispered words. 'Did I ever tell you I dreamed of owning a garage, doc? I was always good with machinery, but I left the farm for the city and a fresh-faced lass.'

His wife patted his hand tenderly.

'A romance that will see you out,' Uncle Z said.

'Hustle me out, more likely,' he retorted. 'Before I could turn around, she got pregnant with our first,' he said, looking up at his wife.

'You never could say no, Olyce. That's your problem.'

Olyce smiled, revealing teeth like rows of rotting tombstones. 'I got me pride, doc.' Olyce was indeed a proud man, who wished to care for his family without the government's help.

The Parps belonged to a fascinating group making a come-back: the very poor. In those days, the very poor often had huge families. The state housed them – reluctantly, as they never paid rent because they had no income – in three areas of the city. The police approved of this arrangement because it simplified raids. The army had built houses in one of these areas, Quarry's Rim, one hundred and fifty years ago for the last officers garrisoned on a nearby penal island. The Parp chil-dren, all thirteen of them, slept on mattresses on the floor and ate their meals in the one long, large room that comprised the ex-barracks. A fire in the middle threw off a little heat and a lot of smoke. A copper for washing clothes stood at one end of the room, a tiny sleeping alcove barely large enough for the parental bed at the other.

The sounds of childish exuberance shot through the window, causing Olyce to start. His puffing became agitated. 'It's quieter in gaol, doc,' he said. He looked like a robin, with his large black eyes, small pointed face, prominent breast and total lack of chin.

'You're surprisingly fit for a fifty-five-year-old man with so much pathology, Olyce,' Uncle Z concluded, sitting back. The thief was wiry and trim, with not a spare ounce of fat. Uncle Z told me later that, in addition to emphysema from too much smoking, Olyce had an enlarged liver from too much drinking, severe varicose veins from manual work, hernias – probably from lifting too many heavy radio consoles – and a perforated eardrum.

'No good me weighing in like a stud bull,' Olyce grumbled, darting a tortured glance towards the window. 'I gotta be agile in me line o' work.'

'Aren't you getting a little long in the tooth for that, Olyce?'

'Yeah, doc, 'course I am, but it's so easy. You'd be surprised how many people leave their kitchen windows unlocked. I have me regulars. There's a nice little Japanese couple that go away like clockwork. They always leave food out, real neat. Something to do with a taboo about an unlucky direction, I found out later in prison.'

The offerings of Olyce's Japanese couple reminded me of Montezuma who, like Hadrian, kept a shrine in the capital in which he collected the gods of conquered nations. We were studying that in school at the time. Some of Cortez's soldiers thought the Aztec island capital was a dream, with its temples and towers rising from the water. Montezuma's fascination with foreign religions caused his downfall. He mistook Cortez for the god Quetzacoatl, returned to fulfil an ancient prophecy of destruction. This paralysed him into inaction when the Spaniards arrived at Tenochtitlan in 1519.

'Amazing what you learn in prison–' Fierce puffing cut short Olyce's appreciation of the virtues of incarceration. He tossed his wife a furtive, tortured glance. 'They say a woman gets worn out from childbearin', but what about me?' Olyce asked. 'She's good for another ten. In fact, she'd love it.'

One look at the robust Mrs P confirmed his statement.

'All I want is to retire,' Olyce rasped. 'Wish I was good at something else that would feed all these mouths. I've really got to hate going into people's homes, like my Japanese couple. I only take what I need, and I try to be neat about it. And I always apologise when I'm leavin', but quietly, to myself.'

A wave of children rolled into the house and crashed against the bed. 'Away with you!' shouted Mrs Parp, brandishing the candle like a weapon. 'Can't you see your father's ill?' There could be no doubt that the woman loved her man.

Olyce peered wanly into the sea of concerned little faces. He turned over, pulling the torn blanket over him. He'd have loved it where I live now, out here in the bush. 'No one to tell you what to do, not wife nor government nor police,' he'd have said.

'I expect Olyce will linger for a few years more despite his poor health,' Uncle Z said as we were driving away.

To our surprise he died shortly after this visit. Sacrifice, a code of ethics and a kind of tragic courage bounded Olyce's life. I could relate to that. Uncle Zoltan said that he never once knew

Olyce to want anything for himself, to bash his wife and children or to complain about them, except for the noise.

Ironically, Olyce's sustained efforts to support his family led to his early death and hastened the intervention he'd worked so hard to avoid. Mrs Parp and the children moved into compassionate housing. The state met all their material needs quite handsomely thereafter, much better than had poor Olyce, with a pension based on number of children.

'I often think of Olyce's honour when called out at night to the welfare young,' Uncle Z has said over the years, 'who treat me like a pizza delivery man.' Some patients seem to think that we provide the same service. Do we? I wonder.

Payback in the Red Centre

Tommy MacDonald

*'Come closer round the fire,' said Tommy MacDonald.
'Aborigines say that white fellas build a big fire and sit far away,
and black fellas make a small one and go close. I've been
fortunate in my medical practice to see the way in which an
indigenous community healed both physical and mental pain.
The physical ailment was appendicitis, the mental affliction was
grief and Kwementyaye was the instrument for both.'*

A WHITE WORM in the belly,' said the ***nungkari***.
'Appendicitis,' I said.

Both the traditional healer and I agreed that something was wrong in Kwementyaye's belly. I've got to call him Kwementyaye because he's dead and people don't refer to the dead by name in central Australia. It's Kwementyaye instead, pronounced Common Jay.

How different this case of appendicitis was from the suspected one I'd seen on the *HMAS Hawke* out at sea all those years ago. No ships this time, no desert ships either, just a house in a Namatjira panorama. I came up as often as my commitments to a new partner and children allowed, in the eternal conflict between my own inner needs and theirs. I'd dragged myself up from the depths of my comfort zone again to experience all that is possible, driven by the spirit of inquiry. That's John Berger and that's me.

Ah, the blue sky, red sand, orange rocks and white ghost-gum trees. This time those glorious colours were underscored by the smell of cooking oil, not extra-virgin cold-pressed green-tinged olive, but something cheap, plentiful and the colour of old rope. No salt-spray brine or machine oil or other ship smells, just dust and cooking oil.

The eighteen-year-old patient wore a T-shirt and lay under some blankets on an old bed in the corner. The brick house was bare except for a few mattresses and a television perched on a box on the veranda.

The medicine man wore jeans and T-shirt and bent over the bed. He brushed Kwementyaye with a eucalyptus branch, in a broom-like fashion, from the shoulders down the arms to the hands and from the groin down to the feet to remove the spirit causing the problem. He then tipped some cooking oil on his hands and massaged Kwementyaye's body. He performed a similar ritual, moving down the shoulders and arms and flicking his hands off the patient's hands, then down the legs to the feet. He went over and flicked his hands out the window.

I wore jeans, a T-shirt and a belt and stood back during my colleague's examination. We were both about the same age, early thirties, and I'd made it my business to find out about the local traditional healers. I waited until he'd finished and looked at me.

'Can I go over and see him?' I asked.

He nodded.

I asked Kwementyaye what he was feeling and whether he had pain. I examined him and concluded he had appendicitis. I now had to talk with everybody, first the *nungkari*, then eight young fellows from their teens to their early thirties who were Kwementyaye's skin group. Their doctor–patient relationship is not the kind we white fellas are used to, which is one-to-one or maybe two-to-one if it's a mother and child. The intimacy of the consulting room doesn't exist. Family members, parents, kids and dogs stand around.

I explained what I thought it was and the *nungkari* explained what he though it was. I said I didn't think I could fix him there and the *nungkari* said he couldn't, so we negotiated evacuation. We all had to agree. Aborigines are amazingly resilient to discomfort, they're a marvel. Kwementyaye was sick with appendicitis, but he got up and took a shower. We drove him to the hospital in Alice Springs, where he left his appendix and returned home.

A few months passed and I forgot all about Kwementyaye with the pressing demands of the day. I was seeing patients one afternoon when two men from the community brought sad news.

'Kwementyaye has been killed in town, hit by a truck,' said one. 'Can you help us?' asked the other.

I went into town with one of the elders and brought Kwementyaye back in a coffin. He'd got drunk with a couple of teenaged girls and Jim, an older fella from the community, and stepped off a curb at the side of the highway.

'A road train hit him,' the elder said, looking out the window. Massive head injuries had killed him instantly.

There was a lot of payback, or retribution, with a huge meeting in the community to determine the punishment for those involved. Elders recalled the young girls to the community. They should have looked after Kwementyaye. A big bush camp was set up just off the perimeter of the community. Family members came from hundreds of kilometres away and argued for days about an appropriate form of payback. All agreed eventually that the family members be allowed to focus payback upon the older male present at Kwementyaye's death.

The football oval, just a sand oval, was the scene of retribution. After much singing and dancing, the men led out this fellow wearing just a pair of jeans and carrying a small wooden shield. The fifteen or twenty male members of Kwementyaye's family all moved out with boomerangs and those long wooden clubs with heavy heads called *nullanullas*. They beat the old bloke to the ground and knocked him senseless.

As well as retribution, there was a lot of sorry business for Kwementyaye. When a young person dies the mourning is usually far more intense than for an older person, who may just be taken out to the bush and buried with little public mourning, like Dulcie, Wally's wife. The sorry business for Kwementyaye included a lot of dancing and keening. The women wailing made an eerie sound. People painted themselves with white ash from the fire and some of the men demonstrated their grief by stabbing themselves deeply in the legs and arms. They mourned day and night.

Out there people are buried, not cremated. I accompanied two elders and three other male family members to the graveyard, about three kilometres into the bush and unmarked with stones. They'd used a backhoe to dig a proper grave for Kwementyaye.

They placed his coffin in the grave and covered it with branches to prevent dingoes getting in. There was going to be a further ceremony as part of the mourning process at the end of the year, which is when the initiation ceremonies start to take place. It was quite a privilege to feel part of that community.

The community's reaction was quite different from its Caucasian counterparts. White fellas' law would have interviewed the truck driver and allocated him part of the blame. Here, people didn't blame the truck driver for Kwementyaye's death. In Aboriginal culture, circumstances surrounding the truck driver were irrelevant. What mattered was that those present hadn't taken alternative action to prevent Kwementyaye's death. For instance, they could have driven back to the community or been at the roadside. Survivors have to accept retribution, so the girls were beaten with *nullanullas* about the arms. Not badly, just bruised. I thought one had a broken arm, but we X-rayed it and she didn't. Jim, the old fella, was concussed and needed to have his head sewn up and in fact I was quite worried about him and wanted to evacuate him, but he wouldn't go.

'That should do it,' I said some time later to Jim as I removed his last dressing.

'Can we go with you to the outstation?' he asked.

I had to go out there a number of times to see kids or the men after they had stabbed themselves. It's symbolic in a way because one of the methods of payback is to spear a person. They aim for the front or back of the thigh, presumably because it causes pain but doesn't decommission people.

'Yes, of course,' I said.

'The wife and I, we're moving there,' he said, eyes averted.

There was still some disgrace associated with Kwementyaye's death. One way people deal with discomfort or conflict is simply to move away to another community or to the bush. Jim had now recovered from his head injury and was well enough to move to one of the outstations, still in their country. Two outstations were linked to our community. They were collections of buildings and humpies with bores, generators and tracks leading in and tracks leading away.

Jim moved on because he had to and I do it because I want to. Maybe he wants it and I need it. He was one sort of outcast and I was another. I thought about visiting patients in the outstations, driving through the stars and the radio static towards the smell of smouldering gidgee smoke and the symphony of Great Dane and terrier. Home visits had taken me through all sorts of conditions in all sorts of settings, rural, urban and waterborne and forced me to test my limits. Sometimes the result was ordinary and I wasn't proud of myself. Other times I didn't do too badly. Had I made much of a difference really or just kept the whole apparatus ticking over to pass on to some other poor bugger?

Glossary of Australian words

Currawong. Raven-like black bird, longer with a bigger beak than a raven, found all along the south and southeast coasts of Australia and in Tasmania, *Strepera graculina, fuliginosa* and *versicolor*. Simpson, K and Day, N. *Field Guide to the Birds of Australia* 4th edn. Ringwood: Viking, 1993; p. 268.

Digger. '1. An Australian soldier, especially one who served in World War I. 2. A common form of address in Australia and New Zealand (originating on the goldfields). 3. *NZ Prison*. A punishment cell. [ital *sic*],' *Macquarie Dictionary of Australian Colloquial Language* rev edn. Victoria: Macquarie Library, 1988; p 92.

Echidna. Porcupine-like monotreme, an egg-laying mammal like the platypus. The echidna and the platypus are the only two egg-laying mammals in the world.

Eucalyptus. Commonly called gum trees. There are around 600 species. One, the blue gum, was imported into California in the 1880s and widely planted 'to absorb the "noxious gases" which were then supposed to be the cause of malaria.' Johnson, Hugh. *The International Book of Trees* London: Mitchell Beazley, 1993; p. 213.

Gidgee. A type of wattle indigenous to central Australia noted for making good fires. Reed, AW. *Aboriginal Words of Australia* Kew: Reed Books, 1996; p. 85.

Humpy. 'Any rough or temporary dwelling; bush hut (Aboriginal).' *Macquarie Dictionary of Australian Colloquial Language* rev edn. Victoria: Macquarie Library, 1988; p. 169.

Kadaitcha. Aboriginal manifested spirit that can travel vast distances quite quickly.

Kookaburra. Blue-jay-like bird, about 45cm. The laughing kookaburra (*Dacelo novaeguinae*) is noted for its 'raucous laughter' and is found in the east and parts of the south of Australia. The blue-winged kookaburra (*Dacelo leachii*) has a 'harsh, cackling scream' and is found across the top of the country. Simpson, K and Day, N. *Field Guide to the Birds of Australia* 4th edn. Ringwood: Viking, 1993; p. 160.

Namatjira, Albert. Renowned Australian Aboriginal landscape painter.

Nungkari. Generic word for traditional Australian Aboriginal healer.

Wattle. Common name for acacia tree, of which there are 500 species. The silver wattle (*Acacia dealbata*) is known in England as mimosa. Johnson, Hugh. *The International Book of Trees* London: Mitchell Beazley, 1993; p. 211.

Wattlebird. Squawking member of *Anthochaera* genus, like an over-sized honeyeater, between 26–48 cm. Species are *A. paradoxa* (yellow wattlebird), *A. chrysoptera* (brush wattlebird), *A. carunculata* (red wattlebird) and *A. lunulata* (little wattlebird). They're found in the southern part of Australia and generally have a raucous cackle or squawk, except *A lunulata*, whose voice consists of 'drawn-out, complex song; rapid twitterings.' Simpson, K and Day, N. *Field Guide to the Birds of Australia* 4th edn. Ringwood: Viking, 1993; p. 224.

References

1   Maugham, W. Somerset. *Ashenden*. London: Heron Books, 1968; p. ix.
2   Maugham, W. Somerset. *Collected Short Stories*, Volume 2, Preface. Harmondsworth: Penguin, 1959.
3   Berger, J and Mohr, J. *A fortunate man*. London: Royal College of General Practitioners, 2003; p. 72.
4   *Ibid*. p.74.
5   de Saint-Exupéry, A. *The Little Prince* (translated by Richard Howard). US: Harvest Books, 2000.
6   *The State of the World's Children, 1984*. Oxford: UNICEF, 1983; p. 182.
7   Beers, CW. 'A mind that found itself.' *Medicine in Literature and Art*, ed. Carmichael, A and Ratzan, RM. Köln: Könemann, 1991; pp. 247–51.
8   Alcott, LM. *Hospital Sketches*. Bedford: Applewood, reprint, originally published: Boston: J Redpath, 1863.
9   Fagan, Brian M. *People of the Earth*, 9th edn. New York: Longman, 1998; p. 538.
10 Hardin, Garrett. The tragedy of the commons. *Science* 1968; **2**: 1243–48.
11 Electronic Corpus of Sumerian Literature at http://www-etcsl.orient.ox.ac.uk/
12 Allin, Michael. *Zarafa*. London: Headline, 1998; p. 36.
13 Cronin, AJ. *Adventures in Two Worlds*. London: Victor Gollancz, 1970; p. 25.